He simply took her breath away

Tall, dark and so achingly familiar. She didn't understand the swift, melting attraction that drew her so to this man. It was as if past and present were superimposed in her mind, as if Adam Walsh were somehow playing both parts. His...and her beloved Jason's.

A wave of loneliness swooped down on Molly, piercing her heart like a red-hot dagger. She reached up and gripped the heart charm—the one Jason had given her—running her fingertip over the uneven edge.

Sometimes she felt as if her own heart was just like this bit of jewelry. Broken. Always searching, longing for the perfect match, the missing piece that fit.

But the other half of the charm was forever lost to her. As was Jason. All she had left were a gold heart severed in two, his picture on her nightstand, and her memories.

And a date with a man named Adam Walsh, who would be knocking on her door any minute now.

Dear Reader,

You're about to meet one of the most mysterious, magical men!

Adam Walsh is many things, but none of them is ordinary, as Molly Kincade—and you—are about to find out.

And neither are any of the heroes in American Romance's ongoing series MORE THAN MEN. Whether their extraordinary powers enable them to grant you three wishes or live forever, their greatest power is that of seduction.

We're delighted at your enthusiastic response to the MORE THAN MEN stories and happy we can bring you more of what you want to read.

So turn the page—and be seduced by Adam Walsh. It's an experience you'll never forget!

Regards,

Debra Matteucci
Senior Editor & Editorial Coordinator
Harlequin Books
300 East 42nd Street
New York, NY 10017

Mindy Neff

ADAM'S KISS

Harlequin Books

TORONTO • NEW YORK • LONDON
AMSTERDAM • PARIS • SYDNEY • HAMBURG
STOCKHOLM • ATHENS • TOKYO • MILAN
MADRID • WARSAW • BUDAPEST • AUCKLAND

To Mom and Dad,
For teaching me to make choices and for always
believing I'd make the right ones.
I love you.

ISBN 0-373-16663-X

ADAM'S KISS

Copyright © 1997 by Melinda Neff.

Prologue

Fear clutched at him, a fear unlike any he could recall. He knew who he was—an undercover agent, trained in lethal force with nerves steadier and colder than steel. Jason Adam North. ID number 425.

So why the hell did he suddenly feel life-and-death panic? As if his cover had been blown and the business end of a .45-caliber Colt was cocked and ready at his temple?

He opened his eyes slowly, wincing at the blinding light over the bed.

A hospital bed?

He shifted by slow degrees, relieved that no weapons were actually aimed at him.

Beside him, slouched in a puce-colored upholstered chair, sat Frank Branigan. The closest thing to family Jason had.

"Hey, buddy," Frank said, rising with the fluid grace of a man trained to be light on his feet. "Glad to have you back with us."

"Where am I?" His vocal cords were raspy from disuse.

"Radishire Hospital."

A government facility. Top secret. "Why?"

"You were in an accident."

Hell of an understatement. His body felt as if it had been chewed up and spit out by a bone-crushing machine. No, not a machine, Jason remembered. A redwood the size of a skyscraper. Events filtered back in strange fragments. He'd been transporting some hush-hush package—volatile and dangerous. Not his usual job, but he'd been available, had had no reason to refuse the assignment. It was late. Raining. The wipers scraping against the windshield had barely been able to keep up with the sheets of water.

A dog had darted in front of him. Punchy from lack of sleep, he'd jerked the wheel. The squeal of tires grabbing for traction on slick asphalt echoed in his brain. Once again he saw the steel-hard tendons of his forearms as he'd gripped the steering wheel in anticipation of impact.

He remembered the sound, a split instant of deafening terror. Metal twisting, screaming—the sharp, horrible percussion of destruction as two powerful forces slammed together. Then silence. An eerie silence as if the entire universe had suddenly ground to a halt.

"Don't conk out on me again, son." Frank Branigan's face, sun weathered and etched with worry, finally came into clear focus. He was average in height, late fifties, with snow white hair. The age and hair color gave the appearance of an easygoing guy. More than one perp had found out the hard way that appearances could be deceiving.

Frank had opted for early retirement from the Los Angeles Police Department vice squad and taken a position with the government. The same department that Jason had worked for since right after college. He and Frank had been a team, family, even though there were no blood ties.

Uncomfortable lying flat on his back, Jason reached for the bed rails for leverage.

An arc of electricity sparked from his fingertips. The railing bent as if it were a ribbon of pliable solder.

"Holy smoke!" He snatched his hand back, his gaze shooting to Frank.

God, how am I going to tell him?

Frank's mouth hadn't moved, but Jason heard the words so clearly in his mind they might as well have been shouted.

"Tell me what?"

Frank appeared startled, but recovered quick enough. "I wondered about that. You've been in and out of consciousness. And each time you've answered a question that wasn't asked."

"What the hell are you talking about?" Jason demanded, forgetting for the moment about the bed railings. "How long have I been here?"

"A month."

"No way." How could a person lose thirty days of his life and not know it?

The image of soft, flowing red hair flashed through his mind. He'd kissed her goodbye, his palms cupping the smooth skin of her face. So tiny, so trusting. He'd told her he'd be gone three days, a week tops.

She hadn't asked him where he had to go, had only smiled and cautioned him to keep safe, her fingertips lightly touching the gold charm at her neck and the one at his. "I'll be waiting," she'd said.

Jason felt his heart pump, felt his chest burn as if a raging fire were sweeping through his system. The monitor beside his bed screamed like a car alarm.

"Molly."

"Who?" Frank asked, reaching over to press a button on the machine. The older man waved back a nurse who came running.

But Jason just shook his head and glanced at the mangled bars on the hospital bed. "Are they making these things out of gum wrappers these days?"

He had an idea he didn't really want to hear the answer. Some sixth sense told him something was wrong, very wrong. His body didn't feel like his own. It was as if his insides were shifting, distorting—humming as if he'd stumbled into an electromagnetic field.

Frank hedged. "Maybe explanations ought to wait. You've been in a coma for almost a month. You should rest."

Especially before you get a look at your face.

"What's wrong with my face?" Jason asked. There was that slight jolt of surprise again. Jason ignored it. "Forget it. I'll find out for myself." He attempted to lever himself out of the bed, and his hand came up with a wad of the mattress. Good God, all he'd done was grip the thick material, and it had ripped off in a palm-sized chunk.

He stared at the mass of polyester, then slowly raised his gaze. "Frank? Talk to me."

Frank retrieved a hand mirror, keeping it at his side. "You remember the package you were transporting?"

"What about it?"

"It was a top-secret thing, a capsule containing an experimental chemical substance—not ours," Frank was quick to insert. "Evidently it leaked when your car impacted with the tree. When we found you, you were holding the box. We're fairly certain a small dose penetrated your system, and it's having some, uh, strange effects."

"What kind of effects?"

Frank glanced at the mangled bed rail.

"You mean like giving me superhuman strength?"

"Apparently."

Now that his senses were fully awake, Jason became aware of the awful chatter that filled his mind. A nurse was talking about the stud she'd gone out with last night. Medical terms flitted through his mind, dosage amounts of drugs he'd never even heard of. So why were his thoughts suddenly filled with terminology he knew nothing about? He felt Frank's uncertainty hit him in a wave so powerful it was almost as if he were inside the other man's body.

"Tell me the rest, Frank. I've got the weirdest feeling I can read your mind, and that scares the hell out of me. Talk to me, damn it."

Frank looked extremely relieved when a bean pole of a man wearing a white lab coat and thick glasses breezed in. "Ah, the man of the hour. Jason, meet Malcolm Kitoczynski, one of the Bureau's finest.

Malcolm, see if you can explain the, er, phenomenon to our boy here."

Dr. Malcolm Kitoczynski studied monitors and slapped a pressure cuff on Jason's arm. "It's a little early for explanations. We—"

"I don't give a damn about your incomplete data and petri-dish experiments," Jason snapped, yanking his arm out of the doctor's hold. "Just give me as much as you've got."

The doctor's sandy-blond hairline shifted as his brows arched. "I thought so." He glanced at the bent bed rail and the wad of polyester Jason still had clenched in his fist. "Acute senses, musculature and sensory—"

"Cut the mumbo jumbo and speak English," Jason barked. "Just tell me why this is happening to me."

"Well, I'm not at liberty to discuss—"

"Screw your liberty."

"Jason," Frank warned. He looked at Kitoczynski. "He has a right to an explanation."

The doctor nodded. "The chemical that's entered your system is acting like a neurotransmitter. It's exciting your neurons, transmitting messages, firing electrical impulses from the brain—"

Jason swore and gripped the lapel of the doctor's lab coat. "You're not in your lofty lab, and I'm not one of your highbrow intellectual partners. Break it down in chunks I can understand."

Kitoczynski's hazel eyes seemed to glaze over as he focused inward, his computerlike brain obviously re-

trieving and discarding data, searching for a simpli-
fied theory Jason could relate to.

The doctor adjusted his thick-lensed glasses. "Okay.
Look at it this way. You put chemicals in your body,
uppers, downers, hallucinogens. They do their work
right at the synapses. Chemically they either facilitate
or interfere with the neurotransmitters—"

"That's a little more information than I need," Jason interrupted dryly, his patience hanging on by a
thread. "In elementary language, this stuff is causing
my brain to send weird signals to my muscles and the
like?"

"Basically. It's similar to an adrenaline surge. Your
fight-or-flight impulses are kicking in at a highly elevated rate."

"Will it go away?"

"We need to do more studies. It could put unnec-
essary stress on your heart and—"

"Kill me at the ripe old age of thirty-four," Jason
finished for him, his gut twisting. He'd stared death in
the face many times, but had been too bold and cocky
to give it more than a passing thought.

Now that thought consumed him. And he didn't like
it.

"Perhaps," Malcolm agreed. "We're still trying to
break down the chemicals. Even then, we don't know
if we've got the whole formula."

"What are my odds?"

"I'm not in a position to give odds. What's happening in your brain defies our data to date. At this
point, we're theorizing that the pins in your shoulder
might have been the catalyst that sparked the interac-

tion. Believe me, we're working around the clock to get you some answers. Now that you're awake, though, maybe we can make better progress. We'll want to study your musculatory abilities and your telepathy."

Jason swore and released his death grip on the wad of ticking he still held clenched in his fist.

So they wanted to study the freak. One minute he'd been a man in love, an undercover government agent on the verge of resigning so he could have a normal life, a life with a very special woman. Now he might as well be a circus sideshow.

"I think he's had enough for now," Frank said to the doctor. "Give him some time to digest."

The doctor nodded. As soon as he was out of the room, Jason reached out and snagged Frank's arm. "Not so fast, Branigan. Let me see that mirror."

Frank shifted uncomfortably, his rubber-soled shoes squeaking against the drab tile floor. "I, uh, worked a little with the plastic surgeon. Your face was pretty messed up in the accident. Although I was marginally attached to the old mug, the new one's not so bad."

The attempt at humor fell flat.

In silence, Jason held out his hand. He was scared out of his mind, and that fear was about to develop into a full-blown rage.

"Have a care," Frank cautioned, holding the mirror just out of reach. "Don't crush the damned thing."

Jason made a concentrated effort to gentle his grip as he accepted the mirror. So far so good. The plastic didn't even dent. Slowly he brought the glass up.

And stared in shock at his reflection.

His eyes were still brown, a shade lighter than his hair and eyebrows. But that was all that remained the same. Every other feature had been sculpted to look like somebody else. Somebody he didn't recognize.

The reflection showed some bruises and some swelling.

And a man he'd never seen before. A stranger.

His world ground to a halt, floundering in an abyss of panic. It would only take the slightest move for that panic to engulf him. He felt the twisting, agonizing pain as his muscles tensed, fought the sensations he didn't understand, the utter loss of control.

The plastic frame cracked as his grip tightened.

Frank snatched it away before it broke. "Hell, son. I thought I did a pretty good job picking out the features. There'll be some scarring, but other than that, you look a little like one of those pretty-boy soap-opera stars."

"I don't watch soaps."

"You know what I mean."

From a purely analytical standpoint, he guessed the strange reflection was fairly handsome. But he didn't want handsome. He wanted familiar. The face he'd lived with for all of his life.

The face that Molly Kincade had fallen in love with.

"Who knows I'm here?"

Frank frowned, laid the mirror aside and picked up an object from the bedside stand. "Just the department heads and me. I wasn't aware there was anyone else to notify." He opened his palm. "We found this in your car. The chain was destroyed."

Jason felt as if the blood in his veins were on fire. He reached out, took the gold-heart charm and gently closed his fingers around it, taking great care not to mangle it as he'd done with the bed rail. And that's when he made his decision.

"I'll give you a telephone number," he said, swallowing heavily against the rasp of his vocal cords, picturing Molly as he'd last seen her, her lips swollen from his kisses, her cinnamon eyes still kindled with the passion of their lovemaking.

She was pure and good and touched him in a way no other woman had. He hadn't told anyone about her, not even Frank, his partner, the man who'd raised him like his own son. He'd wanted to bask in her sweetness, hoard her to himself for just a little longer, never realizing that a little longer would turn into forever.

Because now he was a freak, a man sentenced to a solitary life of loneliness. No way could he saddle her with a man whose body and mind could turn on him like a monster.

Molly deserved better than that. But he couldn't let her believe he'd abandoned her. God, what must she be thinking? Did she wonder why he hadn't called? Had she checked all the hospitals? Jason had kept this part of his life from her. He'd told her he was in law enforcement. And Molly had never pried. She'd accepted him just as he was.

Loved him.

The ache in his chest grew, and it had nothing to do with the fresh scars across his rib cage that were pink and tender. Nor did the ache come from the bizarre reaction that charged his muscles and blood to a hyperphysical state.

"How long will I be here?"

Frank shrugged. "Couple of months for recuperation. Longer than that to study these, uh, you know."

"A freak under a microscope," Jason said nastily.

"You were going to give me a phone number." Frank seemed more than ready to escape the room. "I can make contact with whoever you want, but this is sensitive stuff. You know that I won't be able to give details and—"

"Just tell her I'm dead."

Frank drew in a swift breath.

"Look," Jason said, suddenly feeling old and tired. He wanted to be left alone, alone with his thoughts and memories. Alone to map out the rest of his sorry life.

"They've given me a new face. I want a new name to go with it. I'll give the department eleven months— if I even make it that long. Add the month I've slept through, and that gives them a year. A year of my life, such as it is now. Then I want out."

"It's not that easy—"

"I want out." His terse words cracked like the deadly report of a pistol shot, sharp and final.

Frank nodded, his gray eyes filled with sadness and understanding. "I'll see to it."

"Fine." Jason reached for a pen on the bedside table. It bent like a piece of wet spaghetti in his grip. Disgusted, he stared at the pen, then looked up. He wasn't a man to cry, hadn't done so since his mom had left him on the steps of a county facility when he was five years old and never returned.

He felt like crying now.

"Will I learn to control it?"

"We hope." Frank reached in his shirt pocket and withdrew a gold Cross pen. "Try this one."

"You've got more faith than brains," Jason muttered, his voice raw and bitter.

"I've trusted you with my life on more than one occasion. I think I can trust you with my pen."

Chapter One

Molly Kincade touched the gold charm at her neck. She still felt the ever-present sadness of loss, yet the feel of the warm metal close to her heart gave her courage.

And Jason had always praised her courage. For the thousandth time, she wished he was beside her, sharing her passion, teasing her about her stubbornness. Oh, he would have tried to talk her out of being here— after dark—and she would have enjoyed the debate, knowing she'd win, knowing he respected her values and her crazy quests, knowing he admired her determination even though it triggered his protective instincts.

Forcing back the memories, Molly slung her purse over her shoulder, locked the faded blue Honda and started up the cracked sidewalk. A group of teenage boys hung out on the corner under a streetlight. She didn't recognize the kids as any who attended Clemons High, where she taught.

The smell of onions and overheated grease permeated the air that had turned chilly for March. Two alley cats had faced off, their ears flattened and tails swishing slowly back and forth.

Even the four-legged animals in this area took to the motto Survival Of The Fittest—or meanest. Everyone seemed determined to fight for his or her own piece of turf.

The rusted hinges of the iron gate leading to the darkened courtyard of the run-down apartment complex screamed in protest as she pushed them open. A baby was crying for his mama in the open doorway of number 212. A man and woman were engaged in a shouting match in the unit next to it. Molly ignored both scenes.

She was here for Lamar. She didn't have any business getting involved in the domestic disputes of people she didn't know.

Molly didn't think twice about going into the rougher neighborhoods of Los Angeles. Quite a few of the students she taught in her high-school English classes lived in poverty-stricken areas. They had no choice when it came to their environment.

Molly was determined that they have a choice about their future. And in order to have a decent future, they needed to stay in school.

Lamar Castillo, one of her brightest students, had been absent for four days. Unsuccessful in her attempts to reach his mother by phone, Molly decided to approach the woman in person. If Lamar's parents didn't realize how bright their son was, she would surely enlighten them.

Fifteen-year-olds needed to be in class, not working day and night at a garment factory.

The Castillos lived in 122. Molly hitched her purse more securely on her shoulder and knocked on the door. It took three tries before the door was answered by a dark-haired little girl wearing cotton pajamas and Garfield slippers. The security chain stayed in place. Smart kid.

"Hi, sweetie. Is your mom home?"

The girl shook her head.

"How about Lamar?"

Again the girl shook her head. Molly frowned. She knew all about latchkey kids. She'd been one herself. Still, this little girl looked too young to be left on her own. Especially at night.

"I'm Miss Kincade. Lamar's teacher."

A smile climbed the little girl's cheeks, producing a dimple. "Lamar talks about you. He said you're a nice lady. I'm Lizzy."

"How old are you, Lizzy?"

"Ten."

"Is someone staying with you?"

The smile vanished as quickly as it had appeared, replaced by a wariness Molly was way too familiar with.

"I don't need no baby-sitter." The little girl stuck out her chin and tapped the toe of her fuzzy animal slipper.

"I'm sure you don't. What time will Lamar or your mom be home?"

Lizzy shrugged. "Probably pretty soon. But I gotta shut the door now, and you can't come in. I'll tell Lamar you was here."

The door started to close. Molly could have pushed it open and insisted on waiting, but the fear behind Lizzy's bravado stopped her.

"Tell Lamar I'll expect to see him in class tomorrow," she called just before the door eased shut. At least three locks could be heard clicking in place.

Her mission derailed for the evening, Molly made her way back out into the courtyard, narrowly missing a tricycle with a broken wheel as she turned the corner. Somehow she had to get through to this family. Lamar had a mind that absorbed knowledge like a sponge. Failure was not an option she would entertain.

When she looked up, her heart thudded. The boys who'd been standing on the corner earlier were now inside the iron gate, blocking it. A single glance told her a lock had been threaded through the fastener.

A lock that hadn't been there before.

Belatedly her street-smart antennae—honed over the years—shot up as she assessed the sight before her.

"What's happenin', sweet thing?"

Sweat slicked her palms as she tightened her hold on her purse. But Molly knew better than to show fear. Kids like this would feed on weakness.

"Look, boys," she said in her sternest schoolteacher tone, "I'm not in the mood to be messed with tonight, so if you'd just step aside, I'd appreciate it."

The tallest of the boys snickered. "What if we're in the mood to be messin' with you?"

The boy—obviously the leader of the foursome—took a step forward, and Molly took a step back, her eyes darting to the locked gate. There was little chance that she could scale the thing.

She backed up until she hit the wall. The boys kept coming. The chilly air turned to ice on her skin. Fear sent her heart beating like a jackhammer.

She tried appealing to their sense of family. "Look, don't make me have to explain this to your mothers."

More snickering. An ominous click rent the air like a shot, and the blade of a knife flashed evilly. So much for family values. Fear, barely checked, threatened to swamp her. It wouldn't do any good to scream. Screams in this neighborhood were ignored.

From the corner of her eye, she saw movement.

A man.

Heading straight for them with purpose. The purpose of lending aid.

Oh, no. She didn't want to be responsible for anyone else getting hurt. There were four boys. They might only be teens, but they were strong.

"They've got a knife," she said by way of warning.

He came out of the shadows, radiating confidence. A Samaritan who seemed to forget he was in East L.A. and not Beverly Hills. "Just as well" was all he said. "I'm in the mood for a good fight."

Molly frowned. Four against one wasn't a good fight. It was suicide. "Everything's fine here."

No, it's not! Get out of here. Call a cop.

"Yeah, man," one of the hoods said. "Everything's cool. Beat it."

"Not tonight. And no cops."

Stunned, Molly watched as her rescuer advanced. Didn't the man have any sense of self-preservation?

The snicks of three more switchblades sounded in unison.

The odds were stacked even more against her savior.

The four thugs focused their attention on the tall man, circling like a pack of wolves. Then, like the swift strike of a cobra, the leader of the group made his move, thrusting the six-inch blade in a wide, deadly arc.

It all happened so fast, Molly questioned her eyesight. The man in black balanced on the balls of his feet and kicked out. Moans of pain echoed off the graffiti-covered walls of the courtyard as four knives clattered to the ground, rendered useless in a matter of seconds. She had no idea how he'd done it. He moved like a whirlwind shadow, never even breaking a sweat. With hardly a scuffle, footsteps pounded against concrete as the boys took off running toward the apartment building.

"Are you all right?" His voice barely carried on the night air. He didn't look at her, his intense gaze focused on the retreating boys, his tough body still coiled for action.

Molly wasn't altogether sure she could speak—her heart was beating like a wild beast in her chest. She gave it a try anyway. "Y-yes. I'm fine."

He checked the gate and gave the padlock a yank. Closing his fingers around it, he crushed the sturdy latch as if it were a wad of paper instead of metal.

Terror gripped her, harder and higher than what she'd already experienced, holding her in its unrelenting jaws.

"How . . . ? Wh-who are you?"

Hinges screeched as the gate swung open with such force it bent like an accordion. Molly sucked in a breath, rooted to the concrete.

The man in black gave her an impatient look—a look filled with pain. Had he been cut? she wondered.

"Don't look so shocked, princess. The damned thing's so corroded a two-year-old could have opened it. Come on. Those boys are going to feel their pride smarting pretty soon. No sense waiting around for them to come back with reinforcements. Kids like that are only brave in packs."

He grabbed her hand, pulling her in his wake. The spark of electricity that arced when their palms touched made Molly jerk. She felt the tremor in his hand, like the hum of static friction, as if she'd just run her finger over a taut, magnetic wire—charged. His grip was loose, nonthreatening, as if he feared harming her.

As soon as the observation registered, he dropped her hand, transferring his grip to the bulky sleeve of her red sweater.

"Are you coming? Or do I need to carry you?"

Molly nodded, then shook her head, too dazed to actually speak. Her gaze strayed once more to the iron gate, now propped at a drunken angle against the concrete post. She picked up her pace, following, wanting nothing more than to escape the inner-city courtyard that had turned into an impromptu prison. Yet was this stranger leading her into another realm of danger?

Somehow she didn't think so. There'd been a certain inflection in his voice, his odd touch, that created a surrealistic calm within her.

As if he were an old friend . . . or a lover.

Which was a perfectly ridiculous thought. She took a deep, trembling breath as raw emotions tried to claw their way to the surface. There were no old lovers. None who were alive.

He went straight for her '89 Honda. How had he known which car was hers? Something was terribly wrong.

Molly balked, digging the heels of her tennis shoes into the dew-drenched grass between the curb and the sidewalk. The sleeve of her sweater stretched in his hold, slipping off her shoulder.

The dark stranger glanced back at her, his brows drawn together. Dizziness swamped her—leftover terror from the ordeal. The vertigo nearly took her down when he gripped her waist and hoisted her up, sitting her on the hood of her car as if she weighed no more than a child of two.

"You've done fine so far. Don't faint on me now."

The impatient command snapped Molly back to her senses like the sharp rap of a ruler against a blackboard.

"I never faint! And I don't know who you are, but I insist you stop tossing me around like a rag doll."

"Somebody ought to do more than that. Don't you have any better sense than to be in a neighborhood like this at night? Alone?"

"You're here," she challenged.

"I can take care of myself."

"So can I." Belatedly she reached into her purse for a small can of pepper spray and held it up.

The man confounded her by grinning—at least what ought to have passed for a grin. There was sadness there, a hardness that told her this man had seen more than his share of ugliness.

"A half pint with a half-pint weapon."

Molly's insides somersaulted.

Jason had called her a half pint.

She only stood five foot two, and that was fudging a little. She'd always told him she might be little but she was mighty. But it was crazy to draw parallels between this dark, Neanderthal stranger and Jason. Jason was gone. Forever. A love like theirs had been a once-in-a-lifetime chance. There would never be another for her.

Jason had been her strongest weakness, a man she'd loved beyond all reason, a man with secrets he refused to tell and she'd never found the need to ask about. She'd known so little about him, other than how he'd made her feel—special, beautiful, perfect. With him, she'd been six feet tall, rich in ways money could never buy.

Theirs had been a whirlwind, lightning-bolt type of love. It happened in a flash and burned stronger with each passing moment. Moments that were so very precious and so very short. She'd give anything to hear him tease her again, to feel his lips pressed against hers. If she could turn back the clock, she would have asked so many more questions, found out so much more, held him closer, begged him to stay, to cement their plans, their dreams, before he went off to do whatever it was he had to do.

But she couldn't turn back the clock. He'd been dead for more than a year. Lost to her forever.

Sometimes she imagined she could still feel their connection. And it hurt. Ached like a wound that wouldn't heal, a wound whose scab continually got peeled off each time a memory surfaced.

And memories surfaced daily, the latest one triggered by the simple touch of a stranger in the night.

The man was still watching her. "Decided yet if you're gonna use that stuff?"

"I might." She put her finger on the nozzle of the pepper spray. "Depends on your answers to my questions."

One dark brow raised. "This isn't a polite tea party, princess. There are bad guys lurking in the shadows."

"You being one of them?"

He shifted forward, his strong arms bracketing her body yet not touching. His palms remained flat on the rusted blue paint of the Honda's hood.

"Yeah," he said softly, his raspy voice barely a ripple on the night air. "I'm a bad guy, and you shouldn't ever forget it."

Her heartbeat thumped again, thrilling her, scaring her half to death. The streetlight illuminated his somber features, the sculpted shape of his lips, the high, defined cheekbones. He had a faint scar beneath his eyebrow and another beneath the dimple in his chin. It was his eyes that held her, though. Empty eyes. As if he'd lost all hope and never expected to get it back.

That single, fleeting spark of hopelessness called to her. Molly could never resist a person in need. It was her one true weakness. The need to fix anyone and anything broken, to take them under her wing and infuse them with confidence and direction and meaning. As she'd done with her brother. As she tried to do with her students.

"I don't believe you're a bad guy," she said softly, pleased that her voice didn't tremble.

"What the *hell* is the matter with you?" His hands balled into fists next to her hips. "If you had any sense, you'd use that spray."

"You've already pointed out that I don't have any sense. Not that I agree with you, by the way." She shrugged, and his breath hissed out.

"Go home, little girl."

Now Molly was affronted. "I may be short, but I'm *not* a little girl!"

His sad, dangerous eyes made a slow, thorough pass over her body, lingering on her breasts—the only part of her that definitely wasn't small. She felt herself responding to that look and mentally kicked herself.

She could very well be in grave danger and she was having sexual impulses. Sick!

"Go home," he repeated, stepping back. His shoulders were rigid, his spine straight, as if forcibly staving off a violent bout of chills or a debilitating weakness.

"Wait!" Molly slid off the hood of the car, surprised that her shaky legs would even hold her. She had an idea he wasn't in much better shape. Despite his military stance, he looked as if he were on the verge of collapse. "You never told me your name."

"No. I didn't."

She might have blinked. She wasn't sure. One minute he was there, and the next he was gone. Sure, it was dark, but this was absurd. Nobody moved that quickly or stealthily.

Keys in hand, she slid into the driver's seat of the car and locked the door. She had the oddest feeling the precaution wasn't necessary, that whoever her protector was, he was still watching, waiting to see her safely off.

Her hands trembled as she fumbled for the ignition.

Even stranger yet, she felt a connection to her rescuer. As if he was someone she ought to know.

Chapter Two

Adam was still shivering by the time he made it home. Pumped up and burning one minute, then freezing cold and weak as a kitten the next. It seemed that each time the adrenaline surged, the recovery process was slower. It had lasted a half hour this time. He fought the weariness that made him want to crawl into bed and sleep for a week. He was determined not to give in—not to give up.

Not now. Not after seeing Molly for the first time in over a year.

Adam figured if the unidentified substance flowing through his veins didn't kill him, his blood pressure surely would.

What the hell could Molly be thinking about canvasing the city streets at night? He hadn't intended to get this close to her. He'd only wanted to see her, make sure she was all right. Well, she wasn't all right. If she kept up this do-gooder stuff, she'd get herself killed.

And Adam couldn't allow that.

He'd gone undercover for a lot of assignments in the past, and although he was no longer technically an employee of the government, he knew people in high places who could pull strings and cut through red tape in a matter of hours.

He was more than confident he'd get what he wanted. The department owed him. Big time. Granted, they'd given him the money for this monstrosity of a house and a sizable cash settlement to boot—guilt money, he called it. But there were certain things that money couldn't buy.

He made his way through the cavernous mansion, past portraits of somebody's ancestors that dated back to the 1800s. They weren't his relatives. Hell, he couldn't even trace his family once removed, let alone centuries ago. He'd bought the huge old house as is, with its heavy drapes, spindly furniture and Oriental rugs. The real-estate people had said all the heirs of the old estate were deceased. So, maybe he did have something in common with the descendants of the old guys framed along the staircase walls. He, too, had no blood ties.

He wondered if anybody would care enough to put *his* picture up on the wall when he was gone. Yeah, right, he thought. They could conduct tours, pausing to speculate on the freak. An ex-G-man, unable and unwilling to trust the system any longer. A system that had let a faulty, half-complete experiment be transported as if it were an innocent birthday cake rather than a lethal chemical.

And lethal it might well be. The best technicians in the world couldn't guarantee his life.

Tick tock. Tick tock.

The blood running through his veins may as well have been pure TNT. So what if he had a new face and a new name. What good were those qualities to a dead man?

He touched his hip pocket where the small gold charm rested in a special compartment of his wallet. At least Molly would be provided for. He'd made sure of that in his will.

Still, he had some time left—no telling how much, but some. He snatched up the phone and punched in a set of familiar numbers. He intended to use whatever time he had left to watch over Molly Kincade.

IT WAS A TYPICAL MORNING at Clemons High. Two LAPD officers were already in the office taking a statement from a sullen teen determined not to cooperate.

Molly grabbed the messages out of her box, hoping to see one indicating Lamar Castillo's mother had returned her call. Typically, she hadn't. She pushed through the door of the teacher's lounge and headed for the stack of foam cups next to the coffeepot.

A man, his broad shoulders filling out a tailored suit jacket quite nicely, stood by the coffeepot, his back to her.

"Touch those grounds and you'll get your fingers broken," she warned just as he was reaching for the scoop in the can of coffee. "Anybody around here can tell you I'm the only one who can make a decent pot."

He turned slowly, and the papers in Molly's hand slipped through her slack fingers, scattering over the floor like confetti.

"You!"

His smile made her insides flip. Their knees bumped as they bent at the same time to retrieve the English essays she'd dropped.

His light brown eyes seared her, searching her features as if he were determined to memorize every pore of her skin. She felt her palms perspire as long-forgotten sensations whipped through her, making her feel restless and much too warm beneath her linen jacket.

The blinding, vibrant attraction took her by surprise. She licked her lips, stunned by the fire she saw burning in his eyes.

Had he groaned? Or had she? Slowly, as if it pained him to do so, his gaze shifted downward, staring with a sort of sad fascination at the charm that swung from a gold chain around her neck.

And that's when the guilt slammed into her. How could she be attracted to another man when her emotions were still so tied up with Jason?

For an insane moment, she thought he was going to reach for her. She saw his hand lift then close into a fist against his thigh.

"Adam Walsh," he introduced. "Guidance tech responsible for surnames, *L* through *P*. First day."

"Oh." Her breathing sounded loud to her own ears. "Welcome to bedlam."

"I thought I was at Clemons."

She grinned. "You can call it whatever you want. Take a quick stroll down any of the hallways and get back to me on where you think you are."

"That bad?" he asked, handing her a stack of papers.

"Not really. Most of the kids are pretty great." It unnerved her the way he was watching her. For a split instant, she felt like easing into his arms. Just as quickly, the need for distance rang in her mind like an urgent fire alarm. Both impulses confused her.

A smart woman would opt for distance. And Molly considered herself pretty darned smart.

Slipping the rest of the stray papers back in the folder, she stood. "Well, I've got to run. If I don't get to class before the students, they're likely to hide my books or something."

She saw him glance at the clock. "School's not in session for another forty-five minutes. What about the coffee?"

"Uh, no, thank you. I'm not thirsty." She backed toward the door, feeling like a dork. Where had that zing of chemistry come from? She hadn't reacted to the presence of a male like this in well over a year.

Discounting last night, of course.

"Thirsty or not, I'm partial to my fingers."

She stopped. "Excuse me?"

"You threatened to break bones if anybody touched the pot."

Molly rolled her eyes. "If what I saw last night is any indication, your bones are fairly safe."

The corners of his eyes tightened, making the scar beneath his eyebrow whiten—as if she'd hurt him with her words. The look vanished, leaving Molly to wonder if she'd imagined it.

"Do you have a name?" he asked.

"Oh, sorry. Molly Kincade. Room 3, freshman English." Damn, he was handsome. Too handsome to be a guidance counselor. He'd be better suited to one of those sexy Calvin Klein underwear ads—dark, brooding looks, bedroom eyes—wearing nothing but a pair of skintight white briefs....

What on earth was the matter with her?

Totally flustered, she reached behind her for the doorknob. "Uh, holler if I can be of help." She nearly ran from the room. She'd acted like a fool, which was perfectly ridiculous. She *never* got tongue-tied around men.

Racing through the office, she skirted other teachers, attendance clerks and the principal. Jody Nance, an assistant, stuck her head out of the dean's office.

"Molly," she called. "Eddie Martinez has been kicked out of third period again. Since you seem to be the only one around here with any kind of rapport with the kid..."

"Fine. I'll speak to him."

Molly glanced over her shoulder as she pushed through the glass doors of the office and headed across the quad. Adam Walsh was introducing himself around, making his way in her wake.

Great. Just wonderful. Her heel caught in the crack of the concrete, and she almost went down. She barely saved the essay papers from spilling a second time. God, she needed coffee. Strong and black and hot. Her insides were a mess.

Ahead of her, leaning against the lockers just beyond the boys' bathroom, was Eddie Martinez. Little stinker, she thought. What had he done this time to get thrown out of class? Probably just neglected to show up. But he was a good kid—and it was past time he started acting as one.

She slipped up behind him. "Eddie."

He jumped as if she'd opened fire with an Uzi, then turned with a sheepish grin on his face. He was one of the few kids who didn't tower over her five-foot-two height. She only had to raise her eyes about two inches to meet his.

"What's happenin', Miss Kincade?"

"Heard you got kicked out of VanArk's third period."

"Aw, no biggie. Who needs that sissy reading class anyway?"

"You do."

"I ain't no retard."

"No one said you were a retard, Eddie."

"Then I guess I don't need third period." He smirked, obviously figuring he'd made some sort of sensible statement.

Molly gave his heavy, pea green flight jacket a friendly yank, letting him know she meant business. "Eddie, Eddie, what am I going to do with you?"

"Take me home with you?" he asked with such a cute grin she nearly laughed.

"We were talking about third period," she reminded. She wished she could take all these kids home with her.

"I ain't going back there, and you can't make me."

"Doggone it, Eddie, your test scores show you're only reading at fourth-grade level. And if that's not bad enough, you're majoring in detention!"

"I don't read like no fourth-grader."

She raised a brow and pulled a magazine out of her open portfolio. "Prove it. Read something for me."

Eddie looked around at the kids passing by them. "Read what?" he asked belligerently.

"Anything. Just open that magazine and start anywhere you like. An underwear ad will do." Why was she obsessing on underwear ads today?

"I don't like this rag." He thrust the magazine back at her.

"Fine. What do you like? I'll get it for you."

"Lay off, Miss Kincade."

"I will not lay off...Eddie!" Her back teeth ground together when he brushed by her and slipped into the boys' rest room. "You're not pulling that crap on me, buddie."

Determined to get through to the kid, she marched right into the boys' room after him, surprised it wasn't crowded with seniors puffing on a last smoke before the bell rang.

"Eddie Martinez, you don't have a third-period class, and that's not acceptable."

"Hey, Miss Kincade. This is the boys' bathroom!" His face had turned a deep shade of red.

"I can read the sign, thank you very much. Now, you've got a choice. You can take *my* third period or study hall. Decide."

"I'll take study hall."

"Wrong answer. You'll take *my* class. And don't even think about not showing up. I'll hunt you down." She frowned when Eddie's gaze strayed past her left shoulder. She glanced that way and caught a reflection in the mirror.

A male reflection.

To make matters worse, automatic reflex had her whirling around to face him when any woman with an ounce of sense would have kept her back turned.

"Mr. Walsh! Uh, I was just . . ." She waved ineptly, her tongue stubbornly refusing to formulate a coherent explanation. Eddie had taken advantage of her embarrassment and slipped out the door. She did have the presence of mind to call after him, "You better not be late, Eddie!"

She turned back to the new guidance counselor, then slapped her hand over her eyes and groaned. "Mr. Walsh. I apologize for intruding this way—"

"Considering how much of me you've seen, why don't you call me Adam?"

Molly bit her lip to hold back the giggle. She'd raised a brother. The male anatomy was not new to her. And she'd known every inch of Jason's body. Still, this man was a virtual stranger.

"Adam, then." Although she hadn't seen anything. "And I do apologize. I'll just, uh . . . Well, do carry on."

She slapped the swinging door and tried to make a dignified retreat. Bright morning sun rained down on her, heating her face. At least, she told herself that's what made her cheeks burn. What a morning!

Her escape was unsuccessful. Adam caught up with her and fell into step beside her. He made her nervous.

"Why do I make you nervous?"

Molly's hand slipped off the glass door she was about to push open. Adam reached past her and held the door. She barely reached his shoulder, and it was easy enough to duck under his arm. He smelled like morning sunshine, clean and crisp. A difficult image in the smog-filled L.A. basin.

"Who says you make me nervous?

He simply raised his brow. The dimple in his chin deepened when he pursed his lips. This man had some face. A woman could spend a lot of time just staring at him.

She saw his lips quirk.

"What?" she asked.

"I'm glad you like my looks." His shoulder brushed hers as they threaded their way through the milling teens in the hallway.

"Figures."

"Hey, you said it."

"I did not."

"Those brown eyes are a dead giveaway."

"Please. I haven't had my coffee this morning."

"And whose fault is that?"

"My own."

His brow quirked again.

"What? Surprised I know how to accept responsibility for my own shortcomings?"

"Surprised you'd admit it, maybe."

The cheerleaders kneeling along the tile floor of the hallway painting a basketball banner paused to stare at Adam. Molly barely refrained from rolling her eyes. Especially when Adam winked and greeted the girls.

"Watch the flirting, would you. These girls are underage."

"Give me a break, Miss Kincade."

"Gladly, Mr. Walsh." She stopped in front of room 3. "Here's where I get off."

"Hmm. Mind if I come in for a minute?"

She didn't like the sound of that "hmm," but she wasn't about to ask him about it. "Do you think your ego can make it though the door?"

"You've got a smart mouth for such a little thing."

"Call me little again, and you'll be sorry."

"Promises, promises."

Everything within Molly stilled. A distant memory slammed into her—an image of her and Jason amid the tangled sheets of her queen-size bed. She shook her head, chiding herself for her thoughts. Why did Adam Walsh keep unknowingly poking at her memories of Jason?

She put her purse in the drawer of her desk and got out her attendance sheet. "Was there something you wanted from me?"

Adam hitched his hip on the corner of her desk. If she only knew how much he wanted from her. He wanted her body and soul, wanted to draw her into his arms every time her thoughts slipped into the past, every time that achingly sad wave of emotion hit him. As he'd learned to temper his strength, he'd learned to block his telepathy.

Except, with Molly his blocking techniques weren't working. Her thoughts and emotions were so powerful they slid right past his barriers.

It was pure torture. It was also pure torture not to stare. She hadn't changed much in the past year, other than the slightly sad tilt to her almond-shaped cinnamon eyes. She had the smooth complexion of a high-class model. And those lips. They were the stuff of every man's fantasy. He remembered that Molly had always complained about her lips, claiming they were too big.

And if he didn't stop thinking about them, he was going to embarrass himself right here in room 3 of freshman English.

His gaze lowered to the hem of her short skirt, which had ridden up dangerously high on her thigh.

She caught him staring and tugged at the material. "Do you mind?"

He closed his eyes, trying to marshal some control. "You've got great legs, Miss Kincade."

"Careful, Mr. Walsh. In this day and age, a person could get in big trouble for making comments like that." It wasn't a threat, nor did her words carry any heat. Molly had never been one to run to others with a complaint. No, if need be, the little dynamo simply came out swinging, verbally or otherwise. It was an impressive sight to behold. One he'd sorely missed.

"I wanted to talk to you about last night."

She ducked her head, several strands of fiery auburn hair escaping the bonds of the single braid that hung down her back. "What's to talk about?"

"What you were doing there for starters."

"Not that it's any of your business, but since you did lend a hand, I suppose I owe you."

She stopped, her brown eyes meeting and locking on to his. He'd always admired her directness.

"You disappeared before I had a chance to thank you," she continued.

Adam grinned. "Not dousing me with pepper spray was thanks enough."

A dimple peeked out in her cheek when she returned his smile. "I've never used the stuff before. It hasn't been legally on the market for long. If you want to know the truth, I've been scared to death of it. Chances are it'd blow right back in my face, and then I'd really be in a mess."

"All the more reason for you to stay out of neighborhoods like that."

She shrugged. "I didn't have much choice."

"We all have a choice, Molly. You made a bad one."

Her cinnamon eyes shot sparks. That was another thing he remembered. Her temper had a short fuse. As quickly as it flared, though, it burned out. Still, he waited for the retort. She didn't disappoint him. Confounded him, perhaps, but didn't disappoint.

"The welfare of my kids is *never* a bad choice!" She reached for a folder and snatched out a paper. "Just look at these scores. Lamar Castillo is one of the brightest students I've ever taught. But he spends more time working in a garment factory than he does in school."

"So you were making a house call to browbeat him into coming to class?"

"I don't browbeat. I've been trying to contact his mother all semester. She won't come to me, so I decided to go to her. Lamar's worth it, Adam. He's got a bright future ahead of him, and I'm determined to see that he has a fighting chance. The problem is, we keep butting heads. I'm determined to feed his exceptional mind, and he's equally determined to feed his family.''

"Yeah, well, my determination can probably outmatch the both of you."

"Ooh, the pretty boy's passionate about something?"

"You're damned right. I'm *passionate* about seeing to it that you remain safe, and I remain sane, and everybody else stays in one piece. And that's a hell of a tough thing to do when you insist on venturing into rough neighborhoods."

Molly frowned. "Who appointed you my knight in shining armor?"

"My armor's tarnished as hell, princess. Makes it easier to slip through back alleys that way. The streetlights don't reflect off the shine."

"What in the world are we talking about?"

"I'm beginning to wonder. Every time I look at you, I get sidetracked. However, I think we're talking about your nocturnal habits."

"Which are really none of your business."

"So I'm making it my business."

"Why?"

He shrugged. "Doesn't matter. Just stay away from the inner city."

"Sorry. My kids are important to me. I'll go to any lengths if they need me."

"They need you here. In class. Teaching them. You can't very well do that with a switchblade between your ribs."

Molly shuddered. She hadn't wanted to admit how scared she'd been last night. "That was my own dumb mistake. My mind was on Lamar and his little sister instead of on street smarts. I won't make that mistake again."

"No, you won't. Because you won't go there again."

She confounded him by laughing. He'd expected her to take him to task for coming on like an arrogant prig. He should have known. Molly Kincade never did the expected.

"Adam Walsh, you've got a lot to learn if you have any hope of making it as a guidance counselor at this school. The type of kids you'll be dealing with will just blow you off if you come on like a heavy with them. Most of these kids are tough guys. They have to be in order to survive. I'd suggest you work on your technique, or you'll be a total flop."

The five-minute bell shrilled, and several kids came strolling in. Molly raised a brow pointedly at his position on the corner of her desk.

Adam stood. "I'll take your advice under consideration. In the meantime, why don't you let me have a go at Lamar? I'll check up on his files and see what I can do."

"Sorry. You're *L* through *P,* remember? Castillo is *C.* Since we're short staffed, I've got *A* through *F.* You'll get Eddie, though. Martinez. The bathroom boy?" she reminded when he frowned. Her smile inched up a notch. "He's a good kid. Father's a drinker—abusive—mom's too scared to cross him. The system just turns a blind eye. Makes me sick." She shook her head. "He could easily go bad. Actually I wouldn't half blame him. But I'm not going to let that happen."

"You just said he was mine," Adam reminded. "An *M*."

"So he is," Molly agreed. "Still, you're the new guy on the block. I think I'll just watch over your shoulder for a while."

"Funny, that's exactly what I had in mind."

His light brown eyes spoke to Molly in a way that had her insides churning. It was a simple fluke that she was responding to this man. She wasn't interested in another relationship. Never would be again.

"Adam..." She lowered her voice, not wanting the impressionable cheerleaders who were watching with avid interest to overhear. "If you're making a pass at me, I need to set the record straight right away. I'm not in the market for a man."

"You got something against our gender?"

She didn't understand the odd glint in his gaze, as if the answer to his question was somehow life-and-death important. She set aside the fanciful thought.

"No. Nothing against men in general. It's just that I lost somebody not too long ago. When he left... Well, he took my heart with him—or the best part of it. The only room left here—" she placed her right palm over her chest "—is for my kids."

Chapter Three

It was late by the time Molly finally made it out of her classroom. Most of the teachers were already gone, as were the students, except for a few stragglers serving detention.

Carrying her satchel full of papers to grade, she made her way to the parking lot. The faded blue Honda sat alone, looking decrepit and forlorn. No, not totally alone, she realized, noticing the shiny black Porsche a few rows over. Who in his or her right mind would drive an expensive car like that in this neighborhood?

Molly got a firm grip on her envy and pulled out her keys. Was it just the contrast of the Porsche, or did her little car look sadder than usual? It appeared to be listing at a drunken angle.

The closer she got to the car, the more her spirits sank. "Doggone it!"

She'd either picked up a nail, or somebody had let the air out of her front tire. Great. The car had been missing a jack when she'd bought it secondhand. Not that a jack would have done her much good right now.

She'd taken the spare tire out of the trunk when she'd helped Jody Nance move last week.

Her insurance company didn't offer towing service, and on a limited income, applying for an auto-club card was an expense that wasn't in her budget.

She turned, intending to go back inside and call a cab, and yelped when she ran headlong into Adam Walsh.

"Problems?" he asked, steadying her with a hand on each of her arms.

Molly's chest actually hurt from the force of her heartbeat. "Yes, there's a problem. You scared me half to death!"

"Sorry." His hands dropped, and he took a step back. "Flat tire, huh?"

"Looks that way."

"Pop the trunk. I'll get your jack and give you a hand."

"There is no jack." She ignored his thunderous look. She knew she should have the equipment and didn't need him to tell her so.

Good grief, the way the man tossed gates around, maybe she should just ask him to lift her car and unscrew the lug nuts.

She saw his jaw tighten, saw the skin at the corners of his light brown eyes pull taut, making the scar beneath his eyebrow whiten against his tanned skin.

Why did those light brown eyes draw her so? And why did she feel as if she'd cut him to the quick when she hadn't even said a word—except that she had no jack.

"So," he said, his voice dangerously soft, "you want to see the freak perform?"

Molly frowned, confused and a little frightened, an eerie flutter dancing along her spine. "Adam—"

He brushed by her and reached for the front bumper of her car.

Molly felt sick. My God, how had he known her thoughts? A thought that had been purely conjured in jest? Or was it just a fluke?

Hands trembling, she reached for him, laying her fingertips against the rock-hard muscles beneath his suit jacket. Even through the tailored fabric, she felt that strange hum of tension, the heat.

"Adam, don't." Who was this man? she wondered. This man who could frustrate her, unnerve her and make her care so easily. Care in a way she hadn't done in a long time... since Jason.

His breath hissed out as he straightened. Hands clenched at his sides, he looked heavenward, as if searching for a measure of fortitude—or an elusive answer he didn't expect to find.

Molly had an urge to wrap him in her arms, to promise him those answers—whatever they may be. He seemed to be engaged in some sort of inner struggle, a struggle he wasn't entirely sure he'd win. A vein at his temple pulsed visibly. Gone was the teasing guidance counselor she'd met this morning.

In his place was the man she'd met last night. The tormented soul whose burdens weighed so heavily it was a wonder he could stand. But stand he did.

Alone.

"Adam?" She didn't know what to say, didn't know how to apologize, or even what to apologize for. "Are you all right?"

He turned then, and the change in him was astonishing. Evidently he'd mastered whatever control he sought.

"Yeah. I'm fine. I've got a jack in my car."

Oh, dear, she didn't want to tell him this. Like a guilty school kid caught ditching class, she glanced away.

"Won't make much difference . . . unless you have a spare that will fit this." She inclined her head toward the Honda.

"You don't have a jack *or* a spare?"

She shook her head. It truly was cowardly not to look at him.

"What if this had happened last night?" he asked softly, slowly, his voice straining with polite patience. "Do you have any idea how incredibly foolish it is to drive with no jack and no spare?"

Foolish. He hadn't called her stupid, but still, the definitions were darned near interchangeable. A flash of irritation snapped her head up.

"Any mission to keep my kids in class is *not* foolish. I go where I need to go and it's been a hell of a long time since someone has had the almighty nerve to try and tell me otherwise." She snatched up her satchel and whirled around.

"And," she stressed as a parting shot, "if I'd had a flat last night, I would have called a cab. Just like I intend to do now."

"Molly, wait."

She looked down at the strong fingers that had wrapped around her arm to stop her departure. He released her almost instantly, but she still felt the heat, as if he were running a fever. The man looked bone tired—which he probably was, she realized. First day on the job at Clemons High would wear out anybody.

As always, Molly's anger dissipated like a wispy cloud in a gust of wind. Her emotions had always been quick to flare and just as quick to calm.

"Unless you've got a spare tire to go with that jack, we're wasting time. I'd like to get home sometime before tomorrow."

"I've got a spare," he said. "But I doubt it'll fit."

"Let me guess. You drive the shiny Porsche over there. The one with the meaty tires?"

"Guilty as charged."

"Too bad."

"Too bad that I drive a Porsche?"

"No. Too bad that the spare won't fit." She chuckled at the image that flashed in her mind. "It's just as well. My little car would probably never again give me a moment's peace if she got to wear a Porsche tire. It'd be sort of like Cinderella's stepsister cramming her foot into the glass slipper. She'd have to give it back because it didn't fit, then she'd be hounding me to buy her pretty things that *did* fit."

She caught a glimpse of the strange expression on Adam's face and laughed. "Don't mind me. I have a wild imagination, and it doesn't always make sense to others."

His features softened. Now the guidance-counselor persona was back.

"Are you anything like your car?"

"How's that?"

"If I offer you a ride home, will you start dreaming of your pumpkin turning into an elegant coach?"

Molly laughed again. "Probably. But I'm tired and hungry and anxious to get home. So if you're offering me a ride, I accept. And I won't even ask you if I can drive."

"You can if you want."

"I'm shocked. A man offering a strange woman free rein with his pride and joy."

"There aren't any material possessions I'd consider my pride and joy."

"None?"

"None."

The bleakness in his tone saddened her. She wanted to ask about it but didn't. She hardly knew this man. Besides, she could identify with sadness that went so deep it wrapped around your soul and threatened to squeeze all the joy from life. She could identify because she'd battled a similar sadness every day.

Every day since a man named Frank Branigan had called to tell her Jason would never be coming back to her.

With a hand at her back, he urged her toward his car and held the passenger door open. Molly settled into the rich leather interior, taking a firm hold on her envy. She had no business dreaming about owning expensive vehicles. No, better to be thankful for the reliable Honda. Not that it was all that reliable at the moment with a bum tire.

The Porsche dipped as Adam slid into the seat. The engine roared to life like the growl of a sleek, powerful animal. She couldn't seem to take her eyes off his strong hands as he shifted into reverse. A gold watch peeked out from the sleeve of his white dress shirt. Everything about this man shouted understated elegance. Well, not totally understated.

"You don't buy one of these babies on a guidance tech's salary," she mused aloud, itching to play with the buttons on the sophisticated stereo system.

Adam glanced at her as he pulled out of the parking lot. Big mistake. Now he was going to have trouble keeping his mind on the road and off Molly's legs. Her taupe skirt had ridden up on her thigh. Even though she had her satchel on her lap, there was entirely too much skin showing for his peace of mind. So close his knuckles could easily brush that creamy skin when he shifted into fourth gear.

He reached up and tugged at the knot of his tie, needing to create distance—as if such a thing were possible in the confines of the sports car. The slight tremor just below the surface of his skin wasn't noticeable, and he didn't feel as drained. Of course, he hadn't really exerted himself. This time he'd been able to beat back the major surge before it consumed him.

"The job's something I do because I care. The money came from an inheritance and sound investing." That wasn't a lie. He'd more or less inherited Jason North's money—government guilt money he'd invested wisely.

"What made you decide on Clemons?"

Hell. This conversation was headed toward a potential minefield. It could explode without warning if he wasn't careful. "I live in South Pasadena. I was at loose ends, and a friend arranged for the interview."

"Oh. Well, good. We're in dire need of staff." She glanced at him, the corners of her full lips tilting upward. "Mind if I give you some advice?"

"I have a feeling you'll give it whether I say yes or no."

She laughed, the sound filling the interior of the car like an exquisite ballad. He'd never known a sound could cup his heart...and squeeze.

"You should lose the suit. Not that there's anything wrong with it. It's great. But the kids'll think you're a stuffed shirt. If you want to gain their trust, you've got to meet them on their level."

He raised a brow. "Any suggestions?"

"A pair of jeans will do. You'll need to turn at the next street," she said at the exact instant he flicked on his blinker.

He saw her fingers tighten on her leather satchel, heard the questions screaming in her mind. He tried to tune out her thoughts, her emotions. It was damned hard with her sitting so close, with the familiar, erotic smell of her perfume teasing his senses.

Molly's heart thudded in her chest, and her palms became slick. He hadn't asked which way to turn. He'd automatically turned left.

"I don't remember giving you directions to my house," she said softly. "So far, you've made three correct turns."

"I saw your personnel file."

"Funny. Those files aren't usually left out for people to see."

His shoulders lifted. She had an idea there was no padding in the seams of that suit. She'd seen this man's strength—even though he'd passed it off as nothing. Now she had to wonder. Her heart continued to pump at an accelerated rate as she waited for his explanation.

"So I snooped."

"Why?" She took her gaze off him for a split instant as he unerringly pulled up in front of her apartment complex.

"Because I was curious about you." He shut off the engine, and for a second the absence of noise seemed deafening.

Molly should have been frightened. She had every reason to be. She'd only met this man twenty-four hours ago. Yet instead of fear, she felt excitement...hope, as if she were standing on the precipice of discovery, of something very important.

Against all reason, she felt the walls surrounding her heart begin to tumble, felt herself falling into this man. Déjà vu, powerful and sweeping, slammed into her. Her throat ached and her heart lurched. It was as if her conscious had merged with his, as if a voice called to her....

A voice she missed so badly.

A voice so like Jason's.

Adam's voice.

"Who are you?" she whispered.

He reached out and ran a gentle finger down her cheek. She felt that touch vibrate in every fiber of her being.

"I'm just a man. A guidance tech at Clemons High."

But why do I feel as though I should know you?

"Don't confuse me with somebody else, Molly."

Unease zinged through her. "How do you do that? You're answering my thoughts." Her world felt ungrounded. The past kept superimposing over the present. Her thoughts and reactions were foolish. Yet she couldn't let it go. Grief warred with fragile hope. A hope she couldn't grasp, couldn't even define.

He shook his head. "I'm answering the look in your eyes. Sometimes people see what they *want* to see. Hear what they want to hear. What they wish."

"But how do you know what I want? What I wish? I—"

His finger lightly covered her lips, lingered for just an instant. "You told me you'd lost somebody, remember?"

She wanted to grab his finger, hold it against her lips for a little longer. But he'd already pulled back. What in the world was wrong with her? He wasn't Jason. It's just that his eyes . . . his voice . . .

"I'm sorry," she said. "I'm making you uncomfortable. You must think I'm some sort of nut."

"No." He reached for the door handle. "I just think the guy you're remembering was one lucky son of a gun. Come on, I'll walk you to your door."

"That's not—" the door slammed shut "—necessary." Before she could gather herself and her belongings, Adam had the passenger door open.

She swung her legs out of the low sports car, and her skirt ended up darned near around her hips. Luckily the satchel afforded her a shred of modesty. She saw the muscle in Adam's jaw flex.

He held out his hand, his gaze darting—for just an instant—to the exposed skin of her thighs. "I'm growing more attached to this car by the minute," he muttered.

Molly accepted his helping hand. His skin was warm but didn't radiate the fierce heat it had before. "If you make any comments about me being short, you might end up with this satchel upside your head," she warned.

"You're little but mighty, right?"

She jerked, her palm tightening around his. Then she mentally shook her head and let him pull her from the low-slung seat. Damn it, she wasn't going to torture herself with those memories. He had no way of knowing those were the same words she'd said countless times to Jason.

Or did he?

She deliberately didn't mention her apartment number, watching to see if he'd make the right turn, find the right patio gate.

"School's out, teacher," he said. "This isn't a test."

"What do you mean?"

"I've already told you I looked up your file. I know you live in apartment 14."

"Darn it, you did it again."

"No, I didn't. Your expressive face shows every thought in your head."

"It does not. And to prove my point, how did you know exactly what it is that I just accused you of doing again?"

"You've lost me."

"I don't think so." He stood to the side as she reached for the latch on her back gate. "Are you coming all the way in to check for bogeymen?"

"I think you can probably manage from here."

"Chicken."

"Excuse me?"

She wasn't going to back down. He shoved his hands into his suit pants, his jacket stretching open. The way he held himself told her he'd already closed himself off from her.

"Adam, there's something . . . special about you. I saw it last night. I've seen traces of it today. You're sensitive to my thoughts, so don't try to tell me otherwise. It's nothing to be ashamed of, you know. Most people consider it a gift."

His breath hissed out on a long, lonely sigh. Molly had the urge to reach for him, to wrap him in her arms and ease whatever caused his sadness.

"That wouldn't be very smart."

Her stomach somersaulted. "Isn't that what friends are for? To offer comfort?" Breath held, she watched for his reaction, unsure why she was so determined that he admit the sensitivity. The thought of someone being able to read her mind gave her the willies, yet at the same time, with this man, it excited her.

She saw realization dawn, saw the scar beneath his brow whiten as the corners of his eyes tightened.

She reached out and placed her fingertips against the steel tendons of his arm. "Maybe you can tell me about it sometime. Not now," she said when when his shoulders went rigid. "But if you need a friend... Well, I'm a pretty good listener."

"I'll keep that in mind." He backed up a step and started to turn. "What time do you want me to pick you up in the morning?"

"Why would you pick me up?"

"Your car," he reminded.

"Oh, damn. I forgot about the tire. Listen, this is probably out of your way. I'll just call a cab."

"Don't be ridiculous. You've just offered me friendship. Isn't that what friends are for? To give one another a lift?"

"I hate it when people throw my own words back at me."

He smiled, and Molly felt something inside her give way. The man was entirely too attractive. And although she'd meant it when she'd told him there was no room in her heart for a relationship, it felt good to at least notice the awareness. She could use a friend. And if the bleakness she kept seeing in his eyes was any indication, he could, too.

"I usually leave around seven. Still, this is out of your way. I might even be able to get the tire fixed tonight."

"You're not going to an empty parking lot alone."

"Adam," she warned. "The quickest way to get me to do something is to tell me *not* to do it."

"Okay, then, go ahead and do it. In the meantime, while you're not doing what I just told you you *could* do, I've got a buddy who can run over and put a new tire on."

Molly had to replay his words several times before they sank in. Her eyes narrowed. "You think you're sneaky, don't you? I've used that reverse-psychology trick on my students countless times. They're usually smart enough to catch on."

"Are they smart enough to accept an offer from a friend?"

"Sometimes."

"Well?" he prompted. "Do I call my buddy or do I hang around here half the night worrying that you'll be flitting off somewhere in the dark?"

"Why should you worry, Adam?"

He stared at her, his eyes straying to the tiny heart charm that rested against her chest. For a minute, she thought he was going to reach out and touch it. A part of her wanted to cover the charm—aside from a photograph, it was the only tangible reminder of Jason that she had left. She had no idea where the other half of the heart had ended up. She'd like to think it had been buried with him. It was more comforting to believe that than to imagine the exact match of her symbolic heart lying abandoned amid the wreckage of Jason's car.

At last Adam raised his eyes to hers, and Molly let out the breath she hadn't realized she'd been holding.

"I'm a worrier by nature, I guess."

"Somehow I don't think that characterization fits you."

He shrugged. "So maybe I'm going through a change or something. Is there any law that says somebody can't worry about somebody else?"

Ah, she thought. The macho ego going on the defense when threatened by softer emotions. She nearly smiled, but thought better of it. "Not that I've heard of."

"Fine, then," he said shortly. "I'll be here at seven to pick you up." He turned, his hands once again shoved deep in the pockets of his suit pants.

Her heart thumped unevenly as she watched his stride. Something about that gait sparked a familiar chord. Or maybe it was just his sadness she was responding to. He'd called himself a freak earlier. Yet she chose to see him as special. She had an idea he really would sleep in his car, just to watch over her.

"Adam?"

He paused.

"Thank you in advance for getting my tire fixed."

He did turn then, and Molly grinned. "It's safe for you to go home. I've got a ton of papers to grade, and I promise not to step a toe outside until you get here."

Slowly the corners of his lips stretched into a wry smile. "Now, why, I wonder, does this feel too easy?"

Chapter Four

Molly was waiting at the curb when the Porsche pulled into the parking lot of her apartment complex.

"I see you took my advice," she said as she slid into the passenger seat.

"About what?"

"The jeans."

He nodded once and glanced over his shoulder as he pulled out into traffic. "They're comfortable."

What an understatement. The denim hugged his thighs like a familiar lover. And it was entirely too early in the morning to be noticing things like that, Molly chided herself.

He glanced at her, his expression unreadable. "Will you accuse me of sexual harassment if I comment on your dress?"

She grinned. "As long as the comment stops at the dress, you're pretty safe."

His eyes lingered at the flirty neckline of her floral dress. She had an urge to tug at the bust line, but controlled it. The flat, half-heart charm with its sentimental-lovers inscription seemed to heat against her skin as his gaze continued to linger.

"Pretty," he murmured.

"Uh, Adam?" The Porsche was veering toward the curb.

"Hmm?"

"Shouldn't you be watching the road?"

He swore and jerked the wheel. Molly grabbed the seat for balance, her skin tingling where his gaze had rested so possessively. It unsettled her to realize how easily this man could raise her desire—with sharp, heart-pounding swiftness.

"I trust you didn't make any nocturnal visits to the homes of your students last night?" Adam commented.

"If you recall, I was a little short of transportation."

"Yeah. Like that would stop you," he said dryly.

"Shame on you, Adam. I made a promise. And I always keep my promises."

Adam's fingers tightened around the padded steering wheel. Yes, Molly always kept her promises. He knew the only reason she'd agreed to stay put was that she'd responded to his emotions. That was another thing about her. They'd shared a unique closeness in their short summer together, reacted to one another on the same wavelength.

Maybe that's why it was so difficult now for him to block her thoughts. And he'd heard her thoughts last night. She'd worried about him, about his disgust over his condition. Her desire to understand him was nearly tangible. But Molly wouldn't force the issue. She'd wait for him to tell as much or as little as he felt comfortable with.

Well, he didn't feel comfortable at all. She was perceptive enough to guess, smart enough to put two and two together.

She thought he was special. She was used to taking on the troubles of others. Typically she'd want to take on his. But he couldn't let her. Each additional burden chipped away at her, taking tiny pieces of her with it.

He knew she wouldn't agree with that assessment. Still, he had to be more careful. He had to make himself keep a distance—to stick to his original plan to watch her from afar. She was beginning to draw too many parallels between him and Jason North.

Adam parked the Porsche right next to her blue Honda. The front right tire was darker than the other three, shouting its newness.

"What do I owe your friend for the tire?"

She hopped out of the Porsche to inspect her rusted vehicle as if it were a long-lost child. Hell, even her possessions received her vibrant attention. And Adam decided he was an utter fool for envying a damned car.

"Nothing. He owed me a favor." That was a blatant lie. He'd bought the tire—as well as a new spare and a jack—and done the changing himself. He'd had a lot of excess energy he'd needed to work off after being with Molly yesterday.

"Then I guess I owe you, don't I?"

"No."

"Adam. You collected a favor, and *I* got the reward. Now I either owe you money or a favor."

"You can pay me back by promising to stay out of East L.A."

"Sorry. I can't make that promise."

"I was afraid you'd say that."

The hemline of her dress danced in the breeze as they approached the gates that guarded the open quad. The school was built around a center square of concrete that sported an amphitheater. Glass doors led to individual hallways and classrooms. Since it was still early, the security guards hadn't yet unlocked the gates.

"We'll have to go through the office," Molly said, then frowned when she caught a flash of a pea green jacket.

Eddie Martinez. Running as if a rival gang was hot on his heels.

She quickly scanned the surroundings visible through the iron gates, but there were no other students in hot pursuit.

"Adam. Something's wrong." Eddie Martinez considered himself way too cool to show outward panic like this.

"Miss Kincade! Man, you gotta come quick. Polikian's got his hand caught in the mechanical vise over in auto shop."

"Oh, no!" Heart pounding, she started for the office doors.

Adam felt Molly's emotions, the fear, the urgency. And like a speeding freight train, roaring and unstoppable, he felt the surge of adrenaline whip through him, felt the pain and heat and distortion as his internal system went haywire. He didn't bother to fight it, knew it was too late. Instead, he snagged Molly's arm, ignoring the zap of electricity that arced between them, and shoved right through the iron gates.

"Dude," Eddie drawled, his dark eyes wide with both awe and a panic he couldn't quite mask, "how'd you do that?"

"It wasn't locked." His voice deepened, became raspy. "Let's go."

Molly gathered the folds of her skirt in her hand and jogged after Adam, her insides a mass of screaming questions. She didn't have time to debate whether the gate was in fact locked or not. A kid was in trouble.

It seemed to take forever before they reached the auto shop. A mechanical motor whirred with strain. Shawn Polikian's dark complexion had paled. Tears streaked his cheeks.

Molly raced over and hit the power switch.

"The gear's stuck," Shawn panted, trying to wipe his cheeks on the shoulder of his T-shirt. "I just wanted to fix my radiator...since classroom was empty...and—"

"Hold still," Adam said, supporting the teenager's arm.

Molly pushed in front of Eddie, needing to help and feeling useless. Shawn's hand was clamped between the jaws of the vise—a machine powerful enough to hold an engine block in place. Splotches of blood stained the concrete floor and the tips of Shawn's tennis shoes. There wouldn't be a bone left in this kid's hand that wouldn't be crushed. She had a fleeting thought as to whether he was right- or left-handed.

The pain this child must be in! She glanced around for a pry bar, but didn't see anything thin enough to wedge between the angry jaws of steel. When she looked back, though, Adam was easing Shawn's hand out of its crushing trap. Her knees turned to mush, and her eyes widened.

Eddie, peering across her shoulder, breathed a stunned expletive she'd just as soon he wouldn't. "How'd you do that, man?"

"'Mr. Walsh,'" Molly automatically corrected, her voice trembling, thready. She, too, would like to know that answer.

"Yeah, man, I know who the dude is. Like, what'd he use? Magic or somethin'?"

"No magic," Adam said. "Polikian here just needed to relax. That and Miss Kincade shutting off the power was enough to let his hand slip clear. Come on, son. Let's get you up to the nurse's office."

Relax, my foot, Molly thought. She'd seen his tension, seen the surge of strength that seemed to race through his body, felt the heat and the taut hum of vibration beneath his skin.

She didn't imagine he was on steroids—his muscles were sleek and defined rather than bulky. And although his clothes didn't suddenly split off his body like those of the Incredible Hulk, something odd appeared to happen to Adam whenever he confronted danger or experienced heightened emotions.

Molly considered herself a fairly open-minded person, yet Adam Walsh astonished her. There was something almost...superhuman about him. Which was a perfectly absurd thought. She folded her arms around her middle, trying to hold the confusion at bay.

He turned, his arm around Shawn's shoulders. When his piercing amber gaze locked on to her, Molly sucked in a swift breath. The dark scowl he wore had nothing to do with Shawn Polikian's crushed hand and everything to do with her private speculation.

This man could hear every thought in her head! He might have tried to deny it, but she knew better.

She glared right back at him. "So?" she challenged. *What do you expect? I don't understand any of this. Help me!*

The shake of his head was almost imperceptible. Lightning swift, his scowl eased, replaced by a bittersweet, achingly hopeless look that was almost too painful to watch.

Neither of the boys even realized what had passed between the adults.

"I'll drive Shawn over to the hospital," Adam said at last. "I doubt the school nurse is equipped to deal with this hand. Why don't you pull his file and notify the parents?"

"Do you want me to go with you?" On some deep level she couldn't define, she knew that a hospital was the last place Adam would choose to enter. And fancying herself having an insight into this man—this near-stranger—was ridiculous, Molly thought, mentally rolling her eyes at her own arrogance.

Next thing, she'd be imagining she had ESP, too.

"You wouldn't like it," Adam said, his voice strained.

Damn it! She might have accepted that this man had the gift of thought sensitivity, but it still jolted her when he did it.

"Besides," he continued as if they were having a regular conversation instead of talking in shorthand, "the Porsche only has room for two. Come on, kid."

He stumbled slightly, then righted himself. Molly frowned and took a step toward him. "Are you all right?"

"Fine." The word was terse, barely audible, as if his energy had been drained.

"Are you sure? Adam—"

"Don't fuss, Molly."

She stared at him for a long moment, worried. At last she nodded. "Take care, Shawn," she soothed, running a gentle thumb along the boy's tearstained cheek. "You're in good hands with Mr. Walsh."

Very powerful hands.

EDDIE MARTINEZ MADE IT to third period.

Lamar Castillo didn't.

Oh, well, Molly thought. She'd deal with Lamar's absence later. Right now she needed to restore some order to the classroom.

"All right, guys. Settle down." Half the students in class towered over her—including the girls—but Molly knew how to get tough when the need arose. It didn't happen often. Her students respected her. And she made it a point to return that respect.

A paper airplane sailed across the room, hurled by Jorge, aimed at Terry. It veered off course, and Molly snagged it in midair.

"That'll be enough, Jorge. Terry, sit down." She closed the classroom door after the final bell, but it opened again.

"Manny, you're late."

"I was hurrying, Miss Kincade."

"Yeah," she drawled, watching him strut into the room at a snail's pace. "I can see how out of breath you are from hurrying so fast.

"Eddie," she called, noticing that her newest student was slouched against the wall, inching his way toward the door. "Don't think I don't see you. There's an empty seat right up front. Plant yourself."

"I just remembered an important appointment."

"Sit," she commanded. "You're on my time now."

He shrugged and pushed off the wall. Much hand slapping and swaggering ensued as he made his way to the desk she'd pointed out. Molly ignored the rituals—and the off-color comments volleyed back and forth. Why did these kids feel as though they had to save face over something as natural and good as coming to English class?

"Eddie, you're doing yourself a favor by being here. Not me."

"Yeah, well, it's pretty dumb."

She raised a brow. "Tough guys flip burgers for minimum wage. Keep that in mind." She picked up a slim book from her desk and handed it to Sabrina, who sat in the first desk. "Pass this back to Eddie. We've just started a study on Shakespeare's sonnets. It won't take much for you to catch up."

"Poetry?" Eddie rolled his eyes and tossed a droll grin to his buddies in the next row. "What do we need to study that stuff for? It's not like it's gonna help us be well-adjusted . . . *citizens* or nothin'."

She walked over and placed a finger under his chin, tipping up his gaze. The students erupted with oohs and meaningless advice aimed at Martinez.

"Eddie Martinez," she said softly. "You're a little fraud. You want everybody to think you're dumb, but you're not."

"What do you know?" he grumbled.

"You're smart enough to tell me Shakespeare writes poetry. I only mentioned the author's name. I didn't say anything about the subject."

He shrugged, a reluctant grin creasing his baby-face features. "I still think it's dumb to read the stuff."

Before she could comment, the classroom door opened.

Lamar Castillo walked in. The dark circles under his eyes were a dead giveaway that he'd worked late. But Molly would save that issue and lecture for another time.

She was just so darned thrilled that he'd made it to class. Even if it was ten minutes late.

"Do you have a pass?"

Lamar shook his head, waiting to see if she'd send him to the office for the required pink slip.

Molly's heart did a funny tumble when she noticed Adam standing in the doorway, just behind Lamar.

"Want to see *my* pass?"

The students erupted in laughter, advice and encouragement.

Molly ignored the chaos, her eyes riveted on Adam. His jeans hugged his strong thighs, fueling fantasies that needed very little prompting where this man was concerned. She didn't want to *see* his pass. She wanted him to *make* one. At her.

She had an idea he'd gone to Lamar's house to get the absent student. For her. Everything within her softened. It had been a long time since somebody had cared enough to notice what was important to her. "Thank you," she mouthed.

He shrugged and gave a half nod as if it was no big deal.

Her heart gave an erratic thump. It was a big deal to her. "Lamar, take your seat, please."

"Mind if I stay and observe?" Adam asked.

Eddie groaned.

Molly grinned. "Be my guest. By the way, how is Shawn?"

"Just fine, now." Adam closed the door behind him and walked to the back of the room, rapping his knuckles lightly on Eddie's desk as he passed.

The kid gave him a you're-okay nod. Adam knew most of Eddie's bluster was all for show. He was one of those kids who was everybody's buddy, a kid who seemed to have his thumb on the throbbing pulse of the school. Oh, he liked to give the impression that he was a loner, but there was compassion and neediness in Eddie Martinez, a combination you just couldn't help but respond to.

"So," Molly said, gaining the class's attention. She got Adam's attention, too. Completely. "Eddie here thinks poetry is dumb. How do the rest of you feel?"

Nobody said anything.

Adam glanced around, wondering how she'd handle the silence, wondering if these kids would open up to her.

The fashion police would have a field day in this room, he thought. There was every conceivable mode of dress—young girls in short, tight skirts, their hair ratted, their mouths full of bubble gum, coal-black eyeliner streaking clear out to their temples; boys with sagging jeans and too-large T shirts. The range went from the grunge look to high-fashion Marilyn Monroe—or Madonna, depending on which generation was doing the looking.

And then there was Molly, with her feminine, floaty dress, managing to look sedate and sexy all at once. Her auburn hair fell in soft waves past her shoulders, the ends flirting with the tips of her full breasts.

"Give me a break," Molly said. "You guys are never quiet. If it's because Mr. Walsh is here, rest easy. The same rules apply as always. Nothing you say will leave this room." Her cinnamon eyes met his. "Right, Mr. Walsh?"

"Word of honor," he said, unable to contain an appreciative smile. She was some woman. A half-pint dynamo with more determination and innate integrity than was sometimes good for her.

"Okay. Eddie, enlighten us as to your grievances."

"Man, Miss Kincade. Nothin' like puttin' me on the spot."

"You started it."

"It's not just the poetry. This whole school's dumb."

"You're not into learning?"

He shrugged. "Who cares anyway?"

"I care," Molly said. "Knowledge is the most powerful weapon you can possess. It gives you power and strength. Choose a goal, Eddie. All of you," she said, her impassioned gaze sweeping the room, touching each individual present.

"Reach for a dream. Then absorb as much knowledge as you can and make that dream come true."

"Oh, sure. How are we supposed to care about doing that when all the other teachers around here make everything so tough?"

Half the students in the class were nodding their heads in agreement with Eddie.

"He's right, Miss Kincade," Serita Montessa said.

Adam knew Serita. She'd been sent to him because she was in danger of flunking Mr. VanArk's reading class. Adam had done some research into VanArk's scoring system. Damned near every student was in danger of flunking. There was something wrong with that picture.

"Most of the other teachers don't *care* like you do," Lamar said.

All the kids started talking at once, nodding in agreement. Adam was pleased to note that Lamar was still awake. He'd had to get the kid out of bed this morning. Lamar was probably operating on about two hours' sleep.

Molly held up her hand for silence. "Are you sure we're not just dealing with personality conflicts here?"

"No way," Eddie said.

"Fine, then," Molly shot back. "What would you do to change it?"

Eddie's shoulders lifted beneath his jacket. Most of the students looked to him, as if he were their leader, their spokesperson.

"Come on, Eddie. Put up or shut up. You've got to have some ideas."

"Maybe I do."

Molly walked around her desk, opened the top drawer and dropped the volume of Shakespeare into the compartment. It hit the metal bottom like the shot of a cap gun. Several of the students jumped. Automatic instinct had Adam reaching for a weapon before he recalled where he was—and that he no longer wore a weapon.

Hell, he'd watched her drop the book. Perhaps it just hadn't registered what she was doing. He'd been caught up in her lips, the way they moved, the way they stretched and formed around each word she uttered. Molly's lips were an obsession with him, had been since the day he'd met her. An erotic, gripping obsession.

"Eddie has just changed our lesson plan," she said. "Instead of Shakespeare, we're going to do an essay."

Paper wads and groans were aimed at Eddie.

"Quiet down. Your assignment is to show me exactly what you think is wrong with this school and how you'd go about changing it. You can use any format. Oral, written . . . whatever strikes your fancy."

"Any format?" Eddie asked, sitting up straighter in his chair.

Uh-oh, Adam thought. That spark in Eddie's eyes didn't bode well for school rules and regulations.

"Any format," Molly repeated. "You can pair up or do the assignment on your own."

"How do we know we won't get in trouble?"

This time she hesitated. Then she squared her shoulders. "I'll guarantee it. No reprisals."

Several students started choosing teammates and making plans. Adam shook his head, wondering just where this assignment would lead.

He had to hand it to Molly. When she took on something, she didn't do it in half measures. He'd known she'd be a hell of a teacher, even though he'd never seen her in action. Their time together had been spent during the summer. Eighty-seven days of incredible pleasure, of whispers on hot, sultry nights, moonlight swims in the Pacific Ocean, picnics under the stars. Eighty-seven short days of a love so incendiary, so sweet, it made him ache to remember.

From this distance at the back of the room, he couldn't make out the charm attached to her gold necklace. But he didn't need to see it to know what it was. His memories were vivid. They'd been at the mall, holding hands. When they'd passed the jewelry store, Molly had paused, dragging him inside. Not to look at rings as most women did...

"Oh, Jason, look." Her gaze fell on the two halves of a gold heart. He loved the way her eyes softened, the way her pouty bottom lip glistened as she ran her tongue along it.

"You expect me to wear a necklace?" he teased.

She laughed, the sound surrounding him, making his heart swell. "Heaven forbid that we should offend your macho image."

He could read her like a book, knew she was dying for a closer look at the jewelry. "What's written on the back?"

She flipped the charm over. "It's a prayer of sorts—forever watch over thee and me and keep us safe when we are apart one from the other."

Adam blinked, trying to shake away the image, the memories of how he'd felt that day. Molly had known he was in law enforcement; he'd just never told her what branch. She knew the dangers, though, knew he'd recently recovered from a pipe-bomb explosion that had resulted in crushed bones in his shoulder, necessitating surgery and steel pins to repair the damage. And she'd known he'd be leaving soon. Although he'd already made his decision to take early retirement, he'd told her he just needed to tie up some loose ends, that he'd be back, that he'd explain all about his job then . . . that they'd make plans.

And Molly, in her gentle, no-questions-asked style, had been content to wait.

So he'd bought her that charm because the inscription had touched her so, because it had been so apt.

Now the other half of Molly's symbolic heart rested in a hidden pocket of his wallet. Although he couldn't wear it around his neck, he was never without it.

His gut twisted with an ache so sharp it was a wonder he didn't double over. And that's when he realized that the ache wasn't just from painful memories; it was physical.

His fingers tightened on the metal desk. The writing table bent forward. Teeth ground together, he jerked it back in place and stood.

He needed to get out of here. Sweat pooled beneath his arms and down the center of his back. Memories he ached to revisit but couldn't caused his adrenaline to surge. Hell, wouldn't that be just hunky-dory. Forget himself for two seconds and show the whole damned class what a freak he was.

Thank God nobody had noticed. The desk was a little worse for wear, but it'd pass.

Molly glanced up from where she was having a private powwow with Lamar. She frowned, but he simply waved and let himself out the door.

He stumbled, looked right and left, realized the hallways were empty and sagged against the wall. His blood pounded in his ears, roaring, making him sick.

The ebbing process of this hated phenomenon was getting worse.

THE BLACK-AND-WHITE marble squares in the foyer blurred as he stared at them. Adam didn't think he had enough energy to make it up the sweeping staircase to his bed. Damn, what the hell was happening to him?

Before he could change his mind, he snatched up the phone from the hall table and punched in a familiar set of numbers. He'd sworn he wouldn't do this, wouldn't beg for hope, told himself it was best to leave well enough alone. But that was before he'd stumbled back into Molly Kincade's life.

The line connected. "Put me through to Kitoczynski."

"Your code, please?" a disembodied voice requested.

"Four-two-five."

A series of clicks and beeps sounded. National security. Adam snorted. What the hell was so secret? Half the stuff they worked on in the lab had no definite conclusions.

"Dr. Kit here." Malcolm used the abbreviated portion of his name since few people could pronounce the long version.

"Adam Walsh. How's the research going?"

"Man, am I glad you called. It's going slow. Not good. Damned mice are dropping off right and left. Their bodies are wearing out at an alarming rate under the constant surge of adrenaline."

Adam felt as if his heart had become a lead weight in his chest. Trust Malcolm to leave the kid gloves at home. Damned good thing the doctor worked in a lab. His bedside manner was the pits.

"Sorry," Malcolm said. "I know that's not what you want to hear. There seems to be a higher rate of mortality when alloy is involved. Gave me some false hope in the beginning—especially since we've already removed those pins from your shoulder. But the other subjects—the ones without the steel as a conductor— have since expired."

Expired.

"I wish you'd agree to come back, Jason."

Adam's grip tightened around the receiver. "No. I'll answer your questions, but I'm not coming back." *Unless you can guarantee me a cure,* he thought. "And the name's Adam Walsh." As much as he wanted to be Jason North—*Molly's* Jason North—he wasn't. Never would be again.

"Sorry. I forgot," Malcolm said. "Can you give me anything more to go on here? New symptoms developing? Anything?"

Adam sank down in a chair by the phone, raking impatient fingers through his hair. "Same stuff as before. Feels like I've walked into an electromagnetic field. Pain's getting a little worse. Sometimes I feel as if I can *see* the internal shift. It's not outwardly visible, though. Skin gets hot, burns me, seems to become electrically charged."

"Anything else?"

"Yeah, afterward I get weak as a kitten, drained, knees turn to jelly. Feels like I could sleep for a week."

"How soon afterward?" Malcolm asked, his voice sharpening.

"No set pattern. Sometimes immediately, sometimes half an hour, sometimes longer." Damn it, even *he* knew that information was worthless. And he wasn't a highbrow lab technician.

"Hmm. I'll run some more configurations in the computer."

Adam could tell Malcolm was itching to get back to his research, already visualizing another answer to a puzzle that appeared to have no solution. He heard the thoughts as clearly as if Dr. Kit had spoken them.

"Anything else?" Malcolm questioned. "Small or large, I need to know."

"Not really. The telepathy's getting stronger." Mostly with Molly, but he kept that to himself.

"That's the least of your worries. Mind reading won't kill you. Hell, I wish I could do that myself sometimes."

Kill you. The stark words were said innocently. Adam's teeth ground so hard his jaw ached. Damn it, he didn't want to die. Not now. "Any advice?" he asked tightly, holding on to his emotions by a thread.

"Nothing new. Same as before. Try to avoid stress, emotions that cause panic or fear."

Yeah, right, Adam thought.

"Adam?" A hint of concern and of the previously lacking bedside manner crept into Malcolm's voice. "I wish I could give you better news. At this point, all I can do is reiterate what I said when you left the lab. Get your affairs in order."

Chapter Five

Adam found himself at loose ends when school let out. Molly didn't need a ride home—he'd seen to that by fixing her car. Lamar was back in class, so there wasn't an immediate worry that she'd be charging headlong into East L.A.

At the moment, he didn't have a single good reason to watch over her. Still, he confounded himself by following her.

She sat at an outside table of a quaint cappuccino bar, reading a book.

Alone.

Why hadn't she gotten on with her life? It'd been a year.

He stood a short distance away, watching her. He could tell she wasn't really reading the book she held in her slender hands. He could hear her thoughts. The sadness. It worried him that she'd built such strong walls around her heart, that she'd chosen to linger in the silence of her memories, caring for troubled teens, with little thought for her own personal needs.

Absently he rubbed his shoulder where the doctors had removed the steel pins a year ago and replaced them with a less volatile material. Things might have been different if they hadn't put metal in his body to begin with.

He was so mixed up. He wanted her to find happiness, he really did, yet he was jealous at the mere thought of another man touching her, soaking up her essence, her laughter and stubbornness and sunshine.

Like now. He saw a blond, good-looking surfer guy giving her the once-over. Any minute now the man would make his move.

Knowing he shouldn't, unable to stop himself, Adam approached her table.

Molly's head jerked up when his shadow fell over the pages of her book. Her breath sucked in, and her heart gave several deep thuds that sent blood rushing to her head, making her dizzy.

"Adam." She touched the gold charm at her chest, a habit she hadn't realized she had until just now. For an instant, with the glare of the setting sun casting his features in shadows, he'd reminded her of Jason. Perhaps it was his stance, the way he held himself, or maybe his eyes, eyes so like another set she longed to see again. Or maybe it was just leftover, impossible wishes, a projection of her thoughts.

"Am I interrupting?"

"No." She set aside her book. "I wasn't really reading. Do you want to sit down?"

He drew out a chair and sent a glance over his shoulder at the gentleman with blond hair wearing a Hang Ten T-shirt. Molly arched a brow. She'd known the man had been eyeing her. If he'd approached, she'd have been friendly but firm in her disinterest.

There was really no call for Adam's dog-with-a-bone glare.

"So, what brings you here?" she asked, drawing his attention back before the two men decided to threaten one another with pistols at dawn.

"You mean why do I keep showing up like a bad penny?"

"Oh, I wouldn't call you a bad penny." A dark, familiar shadow perhaps, but not a penny.

"I was on my way home and saw you."

"Where's home?"

"About two blocks south of yours."

"Hmm. Two blocks south of mine is a pretty affluent neighborhood."

Adam shrugged. "I suppose."

"Oh, I forgot. You're the man who takes expensive material possessions for granted."

"I didn't say I took them for granted. Just that there weren't any I'd consider my pride and joy."

That was so hard for Molly to relate to. She'd barely scraped by for most of her life. "I'm fairly certain I don't share your sentiments. If I had money, I'd use it . . . and I'd cherish every belonging, big or small."

A fly buzzed the rim of her coffee. Adam waved it away, the gold watch on his wrist catching the glare of the late-afternoon sun. It was an expensive piece of jewelry, Molly guessed, elegant yet functional with its many dials and gadgets. She almost giggled at the James Bond image that popped in her mind.

Before she could get a better look at the watch, he put his hand in his lap, and the table blocked her view.

"What would you buy if you had unlimited funds?"

"I don't know that I'd want *unlimited* funds. I would, however, buy a house big enough to take in all the kids who are forced on the streets without a choice."

"That'd take a pretty big house."

"Maybe." She corralled a strand of hair that blew in her face and clung to her lip gloss. Adam's gaze tracked the movement, lingering, making her skin heat.

"So, is that your dream, Molly? To run a halfway house for kids?"

"Yes, I suppose it is. It's just that there are so many out there in need."

"True." He pointed to her paper cup. "Your coffee's getting cold."

"It's iced *caffè latte*. Want a taste?" She pushed the cup toward him. When his sculpted lips touched the rim, memory, sharp and swift, zinged her. Memories of a scene just like this, of Jason and her discussing their dreams, of sharing the same cup of iced *caffè latte*.

It hurt so much that tears stung her eyes.

She saw Adam's fingers tighten around the paper holder, watched him carefully place the cup back on the table. Their eyes met, and Molly had trouble looking away. There was something there, something she felt she should recognize. Cars cruised the boulevard behind them and horns blared, but none of this registered.

The moment spun out, enclosing them in a private cocoon, a fantasy bubble where questions might have been asked, answers might have been given. An instant, powerful connection that mesmerized.

A kid on in-line skates whizzed by, skates scraping against the sidewalk. Molly blinked, dragging herself back to reality.

"Sorry. I don't know what it is about you, but you keep poking at my memories." The look that came over him was so familiar. It was a look she'd seen on her own face in the mirror countless times over the past year.

Were she and Adam Walsh kindred spirits? Had he, too, known the pain of loss? A love so deep there could never be another to compare or replace it?

"Do you want me to go?" he asked softly.

"No. I mean, unless you want to. It can't be comfortable for a man when a woman is thinking about somebody else ..." She rolled her eyes, feeling her cheeks flush. "Not that there's anything between us, or that you'd even care that I was thinking about ..." She buried her face in her hands. "Good grief. Don't pay any attention to me. Just forget I said anything."

His strong shoulders lifted. She saw the utter desolation that flashed in his light brown eyes.

Something terrible was eating at this man.

Change the subject, she told herself. She didn't have any room in her heart or her life for the sadness of another man. Teenagers, yes. A man who could possibly have relationship on his mind, no.

She had enough sadness of her own to deal with, thank you very much. And although she sometimes thought she could fix the whole world, she couldn't.

"I'm glad you realize that," Adam said.

Her insides lurched. "I swear I'm going to wear tin foil over my head or something."

She knew the exact instant he realized what he'd done. His lips twisted in self-disgust. "I suppose it's worth a try."

She reached across the table, started to touch him and changed her mind. "I can't begin to understand what it's like for you, but I think you should treat it as a gift."

His gaze focused on the traffic behind her. "It's a gift I'd rather not have."

"Have you always been this sensitive?"

"No. It's a recent development."

She wanted to know *how* recent, but she could see he was about to draw into himself, so she changed the subject. "You said you live in that expensive area south of me. Tell me it's not one of those great old mansions I drool over."

His gaze settled back on her, speculative, probing, making her feel as if there was some elusive detail she'd missed, something she should remember.

"Okay, it's not."

Molly blinked. "It's not?"

"Actually it is. But you told me to tell you—"

She tossed her napkin at him. With his quick reflexes, he snagged it before it hit him in the face.

"I don't suppose you conduct guided tours?"

"I haven't so far. The place is pretty sparse. I haven't been in town long, and I haven't had a chance to do much furniture shopping."

"Your house is empty?"

"Not totally. The previous owners left a few antiques and some pictures of some old guys on the wall."

For some reason, that tickled Molly. "You have pictures of somebody else's family on your walls?"

"Sure, why not?"

Didn't he have family of his own? she wondered. Jason hadn't. Really, though, it was none of her business.

"Speaking of mansions and money," she said before she could stop herself, "there's a dinner dance tomorrow night at the Pasadena Ritz. It's a charity function put on by the Chamber of Commerce. The proceeds will go toward getting our kids off the streets."

"A cause that's close to your heart."

"It's a project I'm very active in, yes. Is there any chance I can twist your arm and get you to buy a ticket?"

"You're a shameless hustler, Miss Kincade."

"For my kids, absolutely."

"Are you going?"

"Yes." Everything within her stilled at the speculation in his watchful gaze. "You could make a donation, or, uh, you could go with me if you wanted." Now, why had she said that? She usually went to these things alone. "It wouldn't be like a date or anything," she stressed.

"It could be," he said, his voice low and intimate.

Goose bumps broke out on Molly's arms, and her heart pounded. She shook her head.

"Do you want my money or not?"

"How much money?"

"More than the price of a ticket." When her eyes widened, he tacked on dryly. "I meant an additional donation, princess."

"Oh."

The corners of his lips tilted slightly. "What time should I pick you up?"

"I could just meet you—" She stopped at the probing look in his eyes. Why was she fighting? If she were honest, she'd admit that she *wanted* to go with him. "Seven o'clock," she said.

"Do I need to go out and rent a monkey suit?"

"You mean to tell me you don't *own* one?" A rich man without a tux? Unheard-of.

"Used to. Don't anymore."

"Then it'd be a good idea to rent one."

ADAM WAS BEGINNING to learn the students' names— at least the ones whose surnames began with *L* through *P.* Funny how he never realized how much fulfillment he could get out of helping kids.

It should have occurred to him. He'd been one of these kids in the system himself, a potential misfit until Frank Branigan had taken him in and made him toe the line, using a combination of Marine techniques tempered with a streak of genuine, no-nonsense caring.

Watching the crowded hallways, he couldn't help but wonder how many of these kids shared a similar background to his. He'd never known his father, and after his mom had left him on the steps of a county home like yesterday's trash, his life had become a seed that just never had the opportunity to germinate and grow roots.

As a boy, he'd clung to the fragile hope of rescue, of his beautiful mother suddenly waltzing back into his life and telling him it was all one big mistake.

But that hadn't happened, and as the years had stacked up, so had his anger. He'd ended up in several foster homes and by that time, he'd been headed on a fast track downhill.

Cocky enough to think he was above average in intelligence, he'd seen little reason to go to school and ended up skipping most of the time. It was while he'd been roaming the streets of Hollywood that he'd accidentally stumbled into the middle of a drug bust.

Being in the wrong place at the wrong time had turned out to be an ironic twist of fate. Frank Branigan, an undercover vice cop at the time, had seen something in the angry kid he'd been and gotten him out of the system, taking him in and teaching him about friendship and choices and consequences.

It was too bad Frank couldn't have foreseen the choices and consequences Adam would one day be forced to confront.

Consequences not of his own making.

Choices painful enough to break even a strong man.

Even a superhuman one.

So, Adam thought, if he'd made the choice to let Molly go, to let her believe he was dead—a fate that could still occur any day now—why was he easing back into her life? Why had he agreed to go with her to the charity function tonight? Hell, he could have just written a check.

He was still grappling for the answer to that question when he felt a tap on his shoulder.

"Got a minute, Mr. Walsh?"

"Sure, Eddie. What's up?"

Eddie's nervous gaze darted along the crowded hall. "Not here, man. Step into my office."

He followed Eddie into the boys' bathroom, remembering the last time he'd been in here, how Molly had brazenly burst through this very door, a half-pint spitfire on a mission, her temperament a perfect match for that rich auburn hair.

"Okay," Adam said. "Looks like your *office* is empty. What's with the secrecy?"

Eddie glared, trying for belligerence. He failed. "I don't rat on friends, but I mighta heard somethin', ya know?"

"What did you hear?"

"Miss Kincade said I could trust you," he hedged.

"She's right, so cut the routine, Eddie. Spill it."

"My sources—who've gotta remain confidential, you understand—tell me Castillo's got a gun in his locker."

"Lamar?"

"Yeah, man. He's been talkin' kinda crazy...and I don't want to see nothin' happen to him. Know what I mean?"

"I know what you mean."

"Good, then. We're straight. You'll handle it...like, *discreetly?*"

"I'll handle it, Eddie. Thanks."

"No problem."

"Hey, Eddie," Adam called before the kid made it out the door. "What's with the camera?" The 35 mm camera hung from a double loop of chain attached to Eddie's belt loop.

He gave a cocky grin and a wave. "I'm not at liberty to discuss that with you, Mr. Walsh. But, hey, maybe you want to shake my hand or somethin'. Never know, I might be famous some day."

Laughing, Eddie unhooked the camera. The length of chain allowed him to bring it right up to eye level. The flash went off like a strobe light.

"Gotcha. Thanks, man." He saluted and strutted out the door, his hips and shoulders dipping in a typical teenage rhythm that shouted *way too cool*.

Adam shook his head and went in search of Lamar's records. Castillo—with a *C* Molly had said—wasn't assigned to him. But it'd be easy enough to look up the kid's locker number.

Armed with the information, he didn't bother to wait for passing period to end. He'd be less conspicuous in a crowd, rather than snooping around the lockers when the halls were totally empty.

He found the top locker and twirled the combination of the lock. Nothing happened.

Damn it, the kid hadn't used the school-issued lock. A dead giveaway that there was something in here he didn't want found.

As Adam reached for the lock again, the five-minute bell shrilled. Great. Now he wouldn't have the cover of a crowd.

"Adam? What are you doing?"

Molly.

He had to give himself points for not jumping. Hell, he was getting rusty. "A little search and seizure—without the warrant. Be a pal and stand as lookout, would you?"

"Lookout... Good grief, what if you get caught?"

He grinned when she actually held up her leather satchel as a shield. So much for being inconspicuous. Her long, silky hair swung in a wild arc as her furtive glance darted right and left.

"You mean what if *we* get caught?"

Molly groaned. "I can't believe you're doing this—*we're* doing this," she corrected. "And why *are* we doing it? No. Never mind. I don't want to know—"

"Could you put a lid on it, princess? You're liable to draw a crowd."

Molly opened her mouth, intending to take issue with his less than charming request, but decided it wasn't worth it. "Just hurry up, would you?"

The sturdy lock busted with a soft click.

She groaned again, refusing to voice the questions that her nerves were screaming.

She really shouldn't have been a party to this, Molly told herself. And she shouldn't have chosen that moment to look.

Sunlight glanced off the barrel of a revolver for a split instant before Adam tucked it under his sweatshirt.

"My God! Whose locker is this?"

With a hand at her back, he urged her away from the bank of lockers. To anyone who cared to look, it appeared that they were innocently heading for their respective classrooms.

"Sorry," Adam said. "That information is confidential."

Molly stopped dead in her tracks and stared at him. Her mouth opened and closed and opened again, but for the life of her she couldn't form a coherent word.

Confidential?

Adam's finger tipped her chin up. Her teeth snapped shut.

"Yeah," he said softly, his sexy lips kicking up at one corner, "confidential."

THE DRESS WAS a simple black sheath with rhinestone straps and low-cut bodice that showed more cleavage than Molly was actually comfortable with. It skimmed her curves, clung in all the right places and ended several inches above the knee. Being short sometimes had its disadvantages. The popular style of midcalf made her look dumpy. Down to the floor, forget it.

But there was nothing she could do about the dress that screamed blatant sex appeal. She didn't have anything else suitable for a fancy dinner. Besides, Adam would be here any minute to pick her up.

She slipped on a pair of four-inch heels, pleased with the added height. The only jewelry she wore was a pair of tiny gold hoop earrings—and the necklace she hadn't taken off in over a year.

Out of nowhere, a wave of loneliness swooped down on her, catching her unaware, piercing her heart like a red-hot dagger. She reached up and gripped the heart charm, running her fingertip over the uneven edge.

Sometimes she felt as though her own heart were just like this bit of jewelry. Broken. Always searching, longing for the perfect match, the missing piece that fit.

But the other half of the charm was forever lost to her. As was Jason. All she had left were a gold heart severed in two, his picture on her nightstand and her memories.

And a date with a man who would be here any minute now, she realized, catching a glimpse of the bedside alarm clock.

She spritzed a hint of vanilla on her wrists and neck, then picked up her purse and shut off the light.

By the time she made it to the back door, he was there, waiting for her. She could see him through the open blinds of the slider.

He simply took her breath away. Tall, dark and so achingly familiar in a black tuxedo. She didn't understand the swift, melting attraction that drew her so to this man. It was as if past and present were superimposed in her mind, as if Adam Walsh were somehow playing both parts. His... and Jason's.

God help her, she was losing it.

He tapped on the glass again, his brows raised in question.

Molly coached herself to breathe and slid open the door. "Sorry about that. I was... admiring you."

"That's what I like. A woman who's direct."

"Now, don't go reading anything into it," she cautioned, both for his and her own benefit. "I believe in honesty. And you, Adam Walsh, do wonderful things for a tux."

"You're looking pretty good yourself, Molly Kincade." His gaze touched on her hair, then slowly lowered to her breasts, her hips, her legs—exposed from midthigh down. By the time he finished his leisurely inspection, every nerve ending on Molly's body hummed.

"That's some dress." His low, rough voice touched her like the erotic whisper of a lover, intimate, exciting... a whisper that threatened to turn her world upside down.

"Thank you." She felt the walls around her heart chipping away. She didn't know how it happened or when; perhaps she'd shivered and he'd slipped past her defenses.

She *did* know that some damage control would be in order if she didn't rein in her emotions.

She was drawn to Adam Walsh, falling... and she was damned scared.

"Don't do it, princess."

"Do what?"

"Break your own creed. I'm not long-term material."

Embarrassment nearly brought her to her knees. It also fired her temper and set her feet firmly back on the ground. She kept forgetting about this man's gift.

"I wish you'd stop lurking around in my head. And if you're going to do it, at least get it right. And...

and . . ." She waved her hand, at a loss for a moment. "And don't take *everything* you hear so literally. I have a tendency to think stuff, then dismiss it."

"Ah, you try on your thoughts like trying on clothes."

"Exactly. Sometimes they fit and sometimes they don't. One day they might feel right, and the next . . . Well, you get the picture. So, cut it out, okay?"

"Sure. Ready to go?"

No! Damn it!

He waited while she locked the door, then ushered her to the car with a light hand at her back.

"Molly?"

"What?"

"Could you think a little quieter?"

Her eyes narrowed as she stared at him. He just stood there, holding the car door open, a slight grin on his face. Finally she slid into the leather bucket seat.

"You better spend an obscene amount of money tonight," she muttered.

ADAM DID SPEND an obscene amount of money. His checkbook ought to be smoldering by now. But what the hell, he couldn't take it with him. Where his life was headed, money had no purpose.

He saw Molly across the room. She'd been keeping her distance. She obviously figured the farther apart they were, the less likely he was to hear her thoughts.

He could have told her it didn't do any good. The connection was too strong. His feelings too deep. None of the blocking techniques he'd learned in the hospital worked.

It was sweet, horrible torture.

It was also torture to watch Molly. Her shoulders were bare, her skin creamy and smooth, unmarred by freckles that most redheads had.

She had a habit of touching and of giving each person she talked to her full attention, young or old. There was nothing phony about Molly. She was pure and good and sweet, with a fiery, determined streak that he both admired and lamented.

He saw her hips and shoulders sway to the gentle rhythm of the music playing. Her innate sensuality was something he doubted she even realized she possessed.

But Adam realized it, and he had a hell of a time not responding to it. She made him want to just pick her up and run with her, to some place private, intimate, a place where the world couldn't intrude, where faulty government experiments didn't exist and where no one mourned and life was guaranteed to last forever.

But there wasn't such a place. His own life wasn't worth a plug nickel—a fact that had been reinforced just yesterday morning.

The damned mice are dropping off right and left. Their bodies simply wearing out at an alarming rate under the constant surge of adrenaline.

As his would.

Malcolm had cautioned against stress, against heightened emotions. With the way Adam felt about Molly, that piece of advice was worthless.

He'd thought he'd grown used to the inevitability of death, talked himself into believing he was comfortably numb, that he had enough willpower to just look but never touch, never allow himself to dream.

Then Molly Kincade had yanked him right back into her life and out of his stupor, bringing his emotions alive in a way that hurt like hell.

He told himself to stay across the room from her, yet his feet moved of their own will, carrying him to her side as the group of people she'd been talking to wandered away.

"Looks like you're doing some pretty good networking," he said.

She turned and smiled, her hips still swaying ever so slightly to the music. "I think the evening's been a success. A lot of money is flowing." The perfect arch of her eyebrow rose. "I got a peek at your contribution. You've been very generous, Adam."

He shrugged. "It's just money. And as you keep telling me, the kids are worth it."

"Oh, come on and admit it. You feel darned good about helping."

"Okay, maybe I do."

"See there, that wasn't so hard." Her grin was like a brilliant sunrise. "There are some great people here, Adam. Instead of standing in the corner scowling, you ought to be mixing. There's even a couple of Hollywood directors here. Any aspirations to be in movies?"

"None." Even though Frank Branigan had teased that he'd had a hand in remaking this face, that it now resembled the face of one of those pretty-boy soap stars.

Molly glanced away, scanning the dance floor. He didn't have to check out her thoughts to know that she was itching to join the lively group. It was obvious.

"Do you want to dance?" Hell, he shouldn't have asked that, knew it would be dangerous to hold her in his arms.

Her head whipped back to his. "Uh, it's getting kind of late...." A dimple peeked out of her cheek when she grinned. "Actually I'd love to."

"I'm a little rusty, but I could probably manage to keep up." The song had a fairly fast tempo. He wouldn't touch her, he told himself, following her across the room to the square of floor where elegantly dressed couples were either stepping in time to the beat solo or paired up doing several versions of the swing.

Molly's enthusiasm preceded her. Her hips were already driving him crazy from the enticing rear view she presented. She almost skipped the last few steps, then turned toward him, moving in perfect time to the beat.

He loved her verve, her lack of self-consciousness, her ability to jump into any situation and turn it into a memorable experience.

"You do a lot better than just keeping up. Do you swing?" she shouted over the volume of the music.

He could have said no, saved himself the agony of touching her, of increasing his yearning for something he couldn't allow himself to have.

Instead, he grabbed her hand and swung her into an outside double turn.

She followed his lead as if they'd been dance partners for years, laughing, enjoying, making him hard and hot and in danger of losing control.

The exertion pumped his blood and fired his senses, scaring the hell out of him. God Almighty, he could crush the bones in her tiny hand if he wasn't careful. This was a mistake. A big mistake.

She seemed to read his discomfort, and that floored him. *He* was the one with the freaky mind-reading abilities.

"You look tired," she said, slowing her pace and smoothing her hands over the lapels of his tuxedo jacket. "Are you okay?" She reached up and traced a finger across the scar at his eyebrow, then the one at his chin. It was hell to stand there and let her do it.

Her gentle touch and compassion did nothing to cool his ardor or the surge of emotions that teetered on the edge of madness, threatening his control. With Herculean will, he managed to corral the fight-or-flight impulses.

The female singer compounded his discomfort by segueing into a slow ballad, a song of inspiration and strength and love, of two people so suited to one another their love could transcend the bonds of time into eternity.

He heard Molly's thoughts, felt her respond to the bittersweet words of the song.

He knew where her thoughts had gone, and the strength of her feelings for the man he used to be humbled him.

Knowing he should step back and doing it were two different things. Before he even realized it, she was nestled in his arms, her hands clasped gently at his neck, her cinnamon eyes gazing directly into his. So easy. So right. Yet so very wrong.

He felt the heat from her body, smelled the hint of vanilla that clung to her skin, agonized over the way the fronts of their bodies brushed, tantalized.

Her moist, slightly parted lips were more temptation than any man should be asked to withstand. And so was the gentle, heartbreaking yearning in her almond-shaped eyes. With a death sentence hanging over his head, would it be so wrong to taste her just once more? Could he take just that much, or that little and walk away? Could he continue the masquerade?

He wasn't sure.

But it was no longer up to him. He *had* to taste her, needed it more than he needed breath in his lungs. He forgot all about the other dancers on the floor, the public setting. Every molecule in his body was focused on Molly. *His* Molly.

Molly saw his eyes shift to her mouth and trembled in anticipation, wondering, wanting when she knew she shouldn't. It didn't seem to matter that there were a couple hundred people in the room. Her world suddenly narrowed to just the two of them, to a longing that was bigger than either of them.

His dark head lowered. Their lips touched.

And just that simply, her entire system jolted, went on alert, eased into the familiar, the achingly sweet familiarity of his kiss, a kiss she'd experienced before, thought she'd never feel again.

She felt Adam's body jerk the instant her thought registered, felt her own breath become trapped in her lungs. Her throat ached and her eyes stung. *Oh... my... God!*

Stunned, she drew back, her body a frozen mass of confusion.

"Jason?" she whispered.

Chapter Six

Adam jerked back as if he'd been jolted by a cattle prod. His emotions were all over the place. Pain, swift and acute, rushed through him like scalding lava, speeding his heart, distorting his senses, sucking away his breath. He was afraid to touch her, afraid not to, afraid the adrenaline surging through his veins would overpower his will, prevent him from tempering this unexplainable strength, cause him to harm her.

Hadn't he already done enough to hurt her?

She looked shell-shocked, like a former POW grappling with the debilitating effects of a torturous flashback.

He couldn't do it. Couldn't tell her the truth.

"You're confusing me with somebody else, princess."

"No." Softly. "No." More strongly this time. "You felt it, too. You read my mind and you reacted."

"Of course I reacted. What man wants a beautiful woman fantasizing about somebody else while he's kissing her?"

She winced as if he'd struck her. People were starting to stare. This wasn't the time or the place. "Come on. Let's get out of here," he prompted.

She followed him without argument. In silence she gathered her purse and her wrap and stood, her shoulder touching his, as they waited for the valet to retrieve the Porsche.

The silence in the car wasn't a peaceful one. Adam was forced to listen to her confusion, her memories, her thoughts—sorting, discarding, hypothesizing, jumping from one possible explanation to the next. He couldn't keep up, couldn't give her the answers or explanations she so desperately wanted.

He couldn't offer her a future.

He wasn't normal.

She deserved children and a man she could share a normal life with, a man she could grow old with.

His altered state prevented him from being any part of that fairy tale, reinforcing his silence.

Like a powder keg on the verge of exploding, he could see Molly's emotions were equally explosive. He couldn't take it, couldn't stand that he was the cause...that his selfishness had inflicted an even deeper wound.

He counted streetlights, trees, license plates, tried every trick he knew to block her thoughts. For once he held on to the disgusting surge that fired his body. If he let go, the weakness would invade. He didn't want Molly to witness that. She was torn up enough already.

When he pulled up in front of her apartment complex, he left the engine running. He needed out. Now.

Needed distance. Didn't know how much more of her hurt and her hope he could stand.

She didn't make a move to get out, so Adam opened his door and came around the hood, easing the passenger door open. He didn't dare give her his hand to help her out.

She stood slowly, searching his eyes, his hair, her trembling fingertips reaching out, brushing the tips of the studs that fastened his tuxedo shirt.

It took every ounce of strength he possessed to step back.

"I wasn't thinking about somebody else," she whispered. "It was you."

He shook his head and broke his own vow, lightly touched a fingertip to her cheek, her trembling lips, hating that he had to lie.

"No," he said softly. "I'm sorry, Molly. I wish I was him, but I'm not."

Her gaze clung to his, begging him to take back the words, begging him to be her dream.

"You better go inside before I forget you're still hung up on some other guy and take what those cinnamon eyes are offering."

She still stood there, staring, making his heart bleed. "Go, Molly."

At last she nodded and turned. He watched until she closed and locked the sliding glass door.

Sweat trickled from his hairline, running in rivulets down his temples. He let out a breath, felt the shift, the nausea, felt the jaws of weakness battering at him, snapping, waiting to trap him.

If he had any sense, a shred of backbone, he'd get in this Porsche and just drive . . . never look back.

Because looking back, wanting, had put them both in a very bad place.

MOLLY STUMBLED into the bedroom, her eyes dry, her throat aching. She picked up the framed picture of Jason, touched her finger to the glass that protected his beloved image, traced the craggy features that were more rugged than handsome. There were no scars marring Jason's brow or chin, no dimple. This man had smiled freely, as he did in the photo.

Her heart cried out as she stared at the photo of the man she still longed for with every fiber of her being. A man with whom she'd shared a love so deep and so open she'd never had to worry where she stood with him.

She remembered the way he'd looked at her with that perpetual spark of amusement in his eyes, as if he were mentally shaking his head at her words, her actions.

That same spark she'd seen in Adam Walsh's eyes.

"Jason," she whispered. "I don't understand. Where have you been? It's you, isn't it? Why? I've got to know!" She closed her eyes, hugged the picture to her breasts.

What had happened to him? Why the new face? The telepathy? The snatches of strength she'd seen that he'd tried to deny?

It was like something out of "The Twilight Zone." But how could she be wrong about a kiss that felt so right?

"He called me half pint," she said aloud even though there was no one to hear her anguish, her hope. "He knew right where I lived. He reacted when I thought about Jason."

What man wants a beautiful woman fantasizing about somebody else while he's kissing her?

She placed the picture back on the nightstand, touched the wedding-ring quilt that still bore the stain of coffee—a spill from a breakfast in bed that had turned playful, then oh, so sensual.

She reached for the light switch, plunging the room into deep shadows, needing the cloak of darkness...to remember, to sort through the similarities, to pick up the fragile thread of a dream she'd never believed she'd dream again, never believed she'd physically hold in her hands again.

And she was certain she'd held that dream in her arms tonight. He called himself Adam Walsh now, and he had the face of a stranger. But a heart didn't lie.

And neither did Adam's kiss.

MONDAY MORNING Molly had a hard time resisting the urge to search the office and hallways for Adam. All weekend she'd vacillated between uncertainty and the cold, biting shock of rage. How could a man she'd thought she'd known so well let her believe he was dead? She'd told herself he had his reasons. Good reasons.

And she'd told herself she *wasn't* losing her mind.

She rubbed her tired eyes and focused her attention on the students, waiting for the classroom to settle down.

Her brows snapped down. "Eddie, where did you get that projection machine?"

"Chill out, Miss Kincade. I just borrowed it. Word of honor, I'll take it back."

His grin was so darned cute Molly just shook her head.

"And the camera?" she asked. "I suppose you *borrowed* that, too?"

"Hey, you want me to do the homework assignment, don't you?"

"I'm almost afraid to answer that."

He grinned again. "I'm figuring you're gonna give me extra credit points. I wrote a paper *and* did this." He pointed to the projector. "Somebody want to kill the lights?"

Serita hopped up to do his bidding.

Images flashed on the darkened chalkboard: a group of girls smoking out in the quad; Jorge Cruz sleeping at his desk; cops busting a kid outside the school gates; a toilet blown off the wall in the boys' bathroom.

She'd told the students to do an assignment on what was wrong with the school. Eddie had gone one better and given them a pictorial record.

The last photo that flashed on the chalkboard sucked the breath right out of Molly's lungs.

Adam. Obviously in the boys' bathroom. Hands on hips, lips cocked ever so slightly, light brown eyes filled with a hint of amusement that still couldn't quite overshadow the loneliness. A loner, so like the majority of these kids in her class.

Where had he been? What had he seen? Who did he miss so desperately to put that loneliness in his eyes?

Me, she thought, her heart thudding deep in her chest, wings of confusion and elation taking flight in her stomach.

Unconsciously she reached up, placed her fingers against her lips . . . and replayed the files of her mind, both recent and distant.

Adam's kiss. So vivid. So uniquely memorable—a kiss that had burned in her memory for an agonizingly long year.

"Miss Kincade?"

Molly blinked. The students were alternately staring at her and at the principal, who stood in the doorway, a piece of paper clutched in his hand.

"My office," Larry Reese said. "Right after class." With those terse words, he disappeared.

"Ooh," several students chorused. "Miss Kincade's been sent to the principal's office."

What in the world? Molly wondered. Larry Reese rarely came out of his office—rarely was even *in* his office, for that matter. The bulk of his job usually fell on Jody Nance's shoulders.

She looked at Eddie. He met her eyes for a second, then glanced away, his shoulders hunched, as if he expected—and was resigned—to being let down.

Molly would have none of it. She marched over to him just as the bell rang and snagged him by the jacket before he could dash out the door.

"I said no reprisals, Eddie, and I meant it."

"Yeah, well, maybe I didn't think. I don't want you to take the rap for me or nothing."

"There won't be any rap to take. I'll see to it. And Eddie?" She gave his neck a friendly squeeze. "You did a great job with the presentation. You've just earned an *A* in my class. Now I expect you to work hard to *keep* that *A*."

SHE REACHED the principal's office the same time Adam did. Everything within her stilled at the sight of him. He was casually dressed in sweatshirt and jeans.

She searched his stance, his features, looking for signs of the familiar, looking for that lost chapter of her life she longed to find again.

His expression gave nothing away. It was as if the kiss had never happened, as if they were just two acquaintances, faculty members who'd only met a week ago. She felt like hitting him, knocking him right out of his complacency, his evasions.

Was she losing her mind? Did she want so badly for him to be that sweet page from her history that she was projecting that longing onto him?

She hadn't heard from him all weekend, had wondered if perhaps he'd disappeared. There was no listing in the phone directory for Adam Walsh in South Pasadena—she'd checked.

But she'd felt the connection, a link that still vibrated and shimmered, making her feel as if he were only an over-the-shoulder glance away. She'd even considered walking the inner streets of L.A., just to see if he'd show up, shadow her, ready to rescue and chastise and play the knight in shining armor—or maybe not so shining. *My armor's tarnished as hell, princess. Makes it easier to slip through back alleys that way. The streetlights don't reflect off the shine.*

Would he have come to her if she'd been in trouble? Would he have somehow known?

Her palms closed into fists to keep from reaching for him. *Please,* she begged silently. *It feels so strong. Are you my dream? Am I going crazy?*

His shoulders went rigid beneath his sweatshirt. Was that pity she saw in his light brown eyes? Was the explanation for his distance as simple as a gentleman trying to save a lady the embarrassment of caring too much when those feelings weren't returned? Was he simply trying to let her down gently because she'd read too much into a single kiss?

A powerful kiss that had tasted of sweet familiarity?

She couldn't abide pity.

She opened her mouth to tell him so, but Larry Reese yanked the door open and motioned them both inside with a terse jerk of his head.

Adam and Molly had barely sat down before the principal tossed a newspaper down on his desk in front of them. It had a note attached, warning whoever cared that this paper had been sent to the *L.A. Times.*

Molly sucked her bottom lip between her teeth, biting it to keep from smiling. The school newspaper showed the same pictures she'd just seen in her class, except they were printed in black and white. The students were probably having a field day with this.

The photos did not show the school in a favorable light.

She met Adam's eyes, saw a similar amusement there.

"What are *you* doing here?" she finally whispered, chagrined that she'd just now gotten around to the inquiry.

He shrugged, acting as if they were just two normal people, as if the uncomfortable moment outside the door hadn't occurred.

"Getting my hands slapped, same as you. Since I'm the kid's counselor, Reese thinks that includes bird-dog duty."

"Eddie's way too slippery to be bird-dogged. He's one of those free spirits, basically a loner who's everybody's friend."

"Excuse me," the principal interrupted. "Can we dispense with the chitchat and get back to the problem at hand?"

Molly turned toward the principal. "So, what's the problem?"

"You can look at this newspaper, this threat to go to the *Times,* and ask me that question?" His voice rose on a note of panic.

"Why not? Looks okay to me. Decent grammar. No misspelled words." She flipped her hair back over her shoulder. "Haven't you ever heard of freedom of speech? It's his constitutional right. And pictures don't lie, Larry."

"I might have known you'd take this route."

She didn't like his attitude. Didn't like the attitudes of half the faculty members at this under funded, understaffed school, for that matter.

"Look. Eddie Martinez has been in my class every day. He's making progress. I assigned this project—perhaps not in this exact format, but I think Eddie showed a lot of initiative. In my book, that earns him an *A*."

She'd told Eddie to fight for what he believed in, and she could do no less than stand behind him. Maybe that credit beneath the photos would spark his pride and change his life.

"What does this—" Reese flicked the newspaper in disgust "—have to do with freshman English? That *is* what you're assigned to teach, isn't it?"

He'd just run afoul of her flash-point, hotheaded nature with that condescending question. By damn, she taught more than English, and he well knew it. The school had her stretched so thin, half the time she didn't know if she was coming or going, much less which doggoned hat to wear.

"It has to do with *learning,* Larry. It has to do with the courage to make a stand! Students will rise to the level of expectation—if we just give them a chance. It doesn't matter if they're underprivileged or undertaught." She was building up a healthy head of steam. If there was one thing that could raise her passion to boiling, it was her students. Her kids.

And the pompous attitude of Larry Reese.

"If you'd quit looking down your narrow nose with blinders on, you'd see that there are some teachers in this school who are masters at underteaching!"

George VanArk was one of them. Head of the English department and determined to flunk every one of his students. It was due to VanArk that she'd even gotten Eddie in the first place.

Thank you very much, George, she thought, *but damn you for kicking Eddie out of class—probably for no good reason other than lack of caring.*

VanArk was an idiot, as far as Molly was concerned, with his caterpillar eyebrows, long nose hairs, grossly hairy ears—he reminded her of Alf the alien on an old TV show.

The instant Molly pictured the crazy image, Adam burst out laughing.

Stunned, all she could do was stare. She hadn't heard him really cut loose like this. The sound, delighted and friendly and unrestrained, filled the dingy office, inviting participation.

Striking yet another familiar chord.

She didn't know whether to laugh with him…or to cry.

Larry Reese stared at Adam as if he'd lost his mind. Nobody had *said* anything funny.

"Alf?" Adam mouthed.

Molly's eyes narrowed slightly. His laughter was uncharacteristic, as was his deliberately calling her attention to his gift. The gift he professed to abhor. Despite her confusion, her brows raised and her lips curved. *Well? Doesn't he?*

"Share the joke?" Reese asked, looking more annoyed by the minute.

"You wouldn't get it," Adam said, his gaze still locked with Molly's.

Molly bit her lips to hold back the bubble of laughter that threatened. She'd been called in front of the principal, and now her *thoughts* had been disruptive.

"Are we through getting our hands slapped?" Adam asked the principal.

"That's not what this is about."

"No? Felt that way to me. You might want to try standing behind your better teachers, like Molly here, instead of worrying over this school's precious image. Face it, Reese, the kid only told the truth. The school's reputation is in the toilet, and it's one step away from being flushed. You'd do better to concentrate your energies on cleaning up that image instead of chastising kids and teachers for pointing out the obvious."

He stood and so did Molly.

Molly was impressed with his speech. It took nerve for a new faculty member to go against the grain like Adam had just done.

Of course, Larry Reese would back down if he knew what was good for him. Clemons was understaffed as it was, and what staff they did have had a tendency to bail out after only one semester.

With her eyes focused on the UCLA letters on the back of Adam's sweatshirt, she followed him from the room.

Other than his outburst of laughter and him backing her up, he'd kept his distance. She couldn't quite figure him out, couldn't seem to mesh the two sides of him—the guidance tech with a soft spot for kids and the superman with dark shadows in his eyes. Had he deliberately played up his telepathy to throw her off track? As a means of making her think he couldn't possibly be her Jason?

If he'd just let her close, perhaps she could—

He stopped suddenly, and Molly slammed into his back.

When he turned, she was stunned by the sparks shooting out of his brown gaze. They fairly singed.

"You might try to fix your kids, Molly, but don't try to *fix* me."

Affronted, Molly simply stared at him for several seconds. The man had more mood swings than Sybil.

"Who the heck are you? Dr. Jekyll one minute and Mr. Hyde the next?" Oh, that was a terrible thing to say. Because she could see in his eyes that he'd taken it literally.

"Damn, Adam. I'm sorry. But I don't know what to think about you, what to expect. One minute you're kissing me like there's no tomorrow, and the next you don't even call. You back me up with the principal, then you turn on me like an angry panther."

"So we're back to the kiss, are we, princess? Just give the word, just one word, that you're not still hung up on that other guy, and I'll be glad to repeat it."

"Would you?"

He stared at her, his spine military straight, his amber eyes intense, probing. She knew he was deliberately searching her mind. And just as deliberately she blocked him. He had entirely too much advantage over her as it was. No sense giving away her game plan.

"I dare you, Adam. I dare you to kiss me."

His breath hissed out, his shoulders slumping as if the burdens he carried were too great. "Do you know what it does to a guy's ego to be compared to another man?''

He wasn't going to give an inch. ''You beat all I've ever seen, Adam Walsh. I'm giving you full permission to take advantage of me, and you insist on being noble. Whatever happened to the old theory about guys on the make who preyed on widows and single women, figuring they'd be an easy conquest because they'd done without for so long?''

He confounded her by grinning. ''I'm not touching that question with a ten-foot pole, not with that fiery red hair of yours and the temperament to match. Besides, we're standing in the middle of the office, in case you've forgotten.''

Molly glanced around, noticing that activity had come to a semihalt. Furtive glances were cast their way, ears straining.

Her mind twisted into a mass of confusion. One minute she felt a certainty so strong she wanted to weep, and the next she felt like the biggest kind of a fool.

Grabbing the sleeve of Adam's sweatshirt, she pulled him out of the office.

Wasn't this just dandy. She'd blatantly propositioned a man and been rejected—in a horribly public setting. She was too stunned by the exchange to even get embarrassed.

He stopped when they were well away from the office and turned toward her. ''I'm not rejecting you, Molly. And I'm not a man on the make. If you knew anything about me, you'd realize that you deserve better than the likes of me. I'm not a good bet.'' He stuck out his hand. "Could you just be my friend for a while?"

She stared at his hand, then shifted up to meet his eyes, eyes that looked so familiar. Slowly she reached out, slipping her palm in his, the thrill of his touch washing over her like a soothing balm.

"I've always been your friend," she said softly.

He nodded, still holding her hand, his eyes shadowed, his touch incredibly tender in a world so tough. She didn't know why she made that comparison, didn't know why she suddenly felt like crying, why she felt so lost, why she felt as if *he* were lost.

At last he released her, then turned slowly and walked away. She waited until he'd disappeared down the hall leading to the auto shop before she let her mind have free rein.

She touched the heart charm at her neck. How could she be wrong about him when it felt so right? There was that certain look in his eyes, the voice, the way he'd called her half pint, the way he'd known where she lived.

She didn't understand the strength, the ESP stuff or the face that looked nothing like Jason's.

But she understood that kiss.

The way he made her feel, how her heart sang when he got close . . . the connection.

She'd loved the way Jason had smiled at her, loved the way his hands reached out for her, loved the power and the gentleness, the certainty that he was her true other half—like this necklace.

And now a man who called himself Adam Walsh was tapping into those same emotions.

It was all so confusing.

But Molly had a determined streak that wouldn't quit. Damn it, her heart knew this man's.

And a heart didn't lie.

One of the first things she needed to concentrate on was wrangling an invitation to his house. She needed to see where he lived, to see if there were any traces of a past she might recognize.

"Watch out, Adam Walsh—if that's who you want to call yourself," she said softly, her words barely audible. "I'm about to turn up the heat, and we'll just see how well you handle it, how long you can hold out."

Chapter Seven

At the end of the week, Molly's frustration level was about at its limit. Adam was avoiding her, and she couldn't seem to corner him.

When the fire alarm shrilled, she had to make a concentrated effort not to sling the eraser against the chalkboard. She glanced at the clock above the door. Ten minutes before the end of the school day. There were no scheduled drills—some kid had probably set off the alarm as a prank. She didn't even try to elicit order in the chaos. There was a major stampede out of the classroom.

Shaking her head, she filed in behind them, knowing they'd lose a good percentage of the students for the day. The kids considered fire drills a sign of freedom, a reason to ditch. They wouldn't stop at the grassy fields and form orderly lines until the all-clear bell sounded. They'd just keep right on going.

The hallways were a sea of bodies, young lovers touching, friends pairing up, girls whispering, excitement racing. A half-eaten apple sailed above the crowd, beaning one of the students on the head.

As if in slow motion, activity stopped.

The crowd parted like the Red Sea, leaving two boys standing several feet apart, glaring at one another. Under any other circumstance, the scene might have resembled two sides choosing off for an innocent game of volleyball, but Molly knew different.

Buddies backed up buddies, squaring off as rivals. And in this school, that spelled danger.

Before she could wade into the fray, it erupted. The two teens charged, their friends closing the circle, forming a human boundary for the tempestuous arena. Girls screamed, boys shouted and off-color language turned the air blue as knuckles pounded against flesh with sickening thuds.

Molly shoved through the fracas, yelling over the din. ''Move! Break it up! Outside where you belong!''

Despite being shorter than the majority of these kids—even the freshmen—Molly felt as if she was making pretty good progress. Single-minded in her mission, she yelped and automatically took a swing when someone lifted her bodily from behind.

Her fist missed, thank goodness—she could get sued for clobbering a student. She stopped struggling when she felt warm breath brush her ear, heard the familiar deep voice.

''Step aside, half pint. You're liable to get yourself killed.''

If she hadn't been so affronted by his caveman tactics, she might have leapt on the fact that he'd called her half pint. But right now she had a more pressing problem.

Adam had both of the fighters by the backs of their shirts. She charged forward, determined to intervene. She couldn't have him tossing these kids through the air.

His head whipped around, the boys suspended, their feet dangling. His tense gaze slammed right into her, pinning her on the spot.

Oh, damn. He'd read her mind again.

Undaunted, she pressed forward, stepping between the boys, still looking at Adam.

"Well, then," she said, her heart still pumping from the near-riot—and from the touch of Adam's hands at her waist seconds ago. "I believe this just about covers fighting in the hallways."

Adam lowered the boys' feet to the floor but didn't release his hold. Still watching Molly, he said, "It's your call, teach. Pardon or punishment?"

Molly glanced at the boys. Tempers still reddened their faces, as did embarrassment. If left untended, there would be retaliation after school. "Jesse, were you aiming that apple core at Manny?"

"No," he said belligerently, his lip split and bleeding. "I just threw it, Miss Kincade. I didn't know the dude was there."

"Bull," Manny said, glaring at his rival.

"Manny, stop it. Cool down and use your head for a minute. Do you actually think anybody's aim could be that perfect in a hallway as crowded as this one? Because if you do, I'm going to do Jesse a big favor and phone the head scout for the Dodgers. Heck, they might even give you a reward for locating a potential pitcher with this kind of talent."

Both boys stared at her with different expressions on their faces. Manny figuring Jesse could never in a million years be a pro ball player, and Jesse entertaining the idea.

Adam gave her a nod of approval. "Everybody cool here?" he asked.

Both boys nodded.

"Perhaps you guys could shake hands?" Molly asked.

Adam gave her a look that suggested she was crazy. She sent the look right back to him. "It wouldn't hurt, you know. Especially since I'm leaning in favor of pardon instead of punishment."

Jesse, who'd done the throwing, stuck out his hand first. He could be big about it since she'd just elevated him to the status of a professional sports star. After a reluctant second, with much glancing around for silent advice from his friends, Manny accepted the peace offering.

"Good," Molly said. "In the future, Jesse, apple cores go in the trash bin. Now, everybody scram."

"Back to class?" Jesse asked.

Molly glanced at her watch. School was officially out in three minutes. "No, but you might at least make a pretense of meeting out on the field. That *was* a fire alarm we heard." Probably a bogus one, but still, rules were rules.

The students dispersed, and it didn't take long for the hallways to clear, leaving only Molly and Adam.

"You've got a way with these kids," he said. "They respect and admire you."

She shrugged. "They know I care."

The clang of a metal door made her jump. She glanced down the hallway and back to Adam. "Now what?"

"Sounded like it came from the auto shop. Would they be closing the roll-up door at this time of day?"

"It shouldn't be open in the first place. Mike Warner doesn't have a sixth period. Maybe we better go have a look."

He took off at a fast clip. "I don't suppose the concept of not getting involved has ever occurred to you?" he asked over his shoulder.

Molly's shorter steps were no match for his longer stride. She had to practically run to keep up. "I might ask you the same thing, seeing as you're leading by a neck."

"More than a neck."

"Oh, I see. We're feeling competitive. You comment on my height again, though, and you've had it."

"I wouldn't dream of it, princess." They rounded the corner, Adam still in the lead. "However, with your determination to wade in where you don't belong, you might think about exchanging those heels for tennis shoes."

"Don't start that where-I-don't-belong stuff again." The sound of a car engine firing to life turned their fast clip into a full-blown race. Without missing more than two steps, Molly snatched her heels off, gaining a burst of speed in her stocking feet.

She heard Adam swear and ignored him.

The first thing she saw when they reached the auto shop was Eddie Martinez, jumping into the passenger seat of the driver-education Nissan. The school no longer had funding for behind-the-wheel training, but the Nissan had become a project Mike Warner used for the auto-shop students.

It appeared Eddie was trying to talk Sebastian out of stealing the car. Had Eddie set off the false alarm as a distraction for a getaway or a plea for help?

There wasn't time for answers to either of those questions right now. Adam was standing dead center in front of the revving car, his hand on the hood. Sebastian, looking paranoid, sweat pouring down his dark temples, gripped the steering wheel, shouting for Adam to move.

The kid looked higher than a kite. He wasn't thinking straight. She saw his determination to escape, saw his fear.

Make the right choice, kid, she prayed silently. *Murder carries a steeper rap than auto theft.*

The car rocked forward.

Molly's heart nearly stopped. "Adam! Get out of the way! Just let him have the damned car!"

Adam never took his eyes off the scared kid. And still, he stood dead center in front of the car.

Molly automatically took a step toward them.

"Stay back." His voice was low and savage, rasping against her nerve endings like an emery board against aluminum, grating and chilling. It was a voice that spelled danger, inspired fear.

Even over the revving engine, the command reached the boys, their eyes growing round.

"Martinez," Adam said, "get out of the car."

Eddie hesitated and glanced at his messed-up friend. "Come on, Sebastian, man. Kill the engine. It's cool.

These wheels are a piece of junk anyway. You don't want 'em."

It was obvious by now that Eddie was an unwilling party to the theft. He was the type of kid who figured he could talk anybody out of just about anything.

This time, though, his negotiating skills weren't doing the job. Molly's hand flew to her mouth as Sebastian slammed the transmission into gear.

She saw the toes of Adam's sneakers grip the concrete, saw the metal hood of the Nissan dent under his palm—a palm that appeared to arc for a split instant. Tires spun, billowing smoke from the wheel wells, filling the auto shop with the acrid smell of burning rubber.

Molly's eyes stung. Eddie and Sebastian gaped. Adam stood stock-still, and the car didn't budge.

It didn't shoot forward to run him down as she'd feared—taking him away from her when she was certain she'd just found him again. Her whole body trembled with horror and confusion. Damn it, there was no way in hell he could explain away this episode.

"Might as well shut her down," he said conversationally, but Molly could hear the thread of pain in his voice. Did it hurt when this happened to him? And what exactly was it that happened to him?

The tires abruptly stopped their revolutions, and the engine died. Eddie leapt out of the car, coughing and waving at the smoke.

"How'd you do that, man?" He was looking at Adam as if he were a hero.

A superhero.

Adam just shrugged and took his hand off the hood, leaning a hip against it where the dent had made spidery cracks in the paint.

"Obviously the transmission's slipping. Probably burned up, by the looks of that smoke."

Both boys glanced at the grayish white cloud and back to Adam, apparently accepting the explanation.

"I expected more from you, Eddie," Adam said. He glanced at Sebastian, who hovered at the back of the car, his gaze darting around as if he expected ghosts to appear and wage an attack. "That kid going to be okay? Do we need to haul him to the hospital?"

"No, man. I've seen him this way before. He'll ride it out."

"You're not his keeper, Eddie. Don't let kids like that bring you down."

Eddie shrugged, uncomfortable. "He ain't got nobody else." That seemed to explain it all as far as Eddie was concerned. "So what are you gonna do about this?" He nodded toward the car, toward Sebastian, then tossed an apologetic look at Molly.

"I suppose since there was no school property removed, we'll pretend it didn't happen."

"I knew you was good people."

"Yeah, well, don't push it, okay?"

"Sure, Mr. Walsh. Catch ya later." Eddie gave a tug to the bill of his backward baseball cap and urged Sebastian out the door.

"That's the second time you've given a kid a reprieve," Molly said.

Third, Adam wanted to say, but he hadn't told her about his discussion with Lamar about keeping a gun in his locker. He didn't intend to. She'd be out to find Lamar like a shot. But he'd made sure Lamar wouldn't get in over his head.

He backed away when she reached for him. Because if she touched him now, he'd want to respond. And he didn't dare do that right now. Not when adrenaline was still surging through his veins. He felt the hum of tension, like electrical currents charging his blood, zapping his muscles, knotting them into ropes of steel. He figured after this bout of exertion, he'd be pumped up for a while. Just as well, as he didn't want her to see the debilitating weakness that would follow. He planned to be well away from her before it hit.

He gritted his teeth against the disgust of Molly witnessing—again—the uncontrollable phenomenon that branded him a freak.

It was an agonizing reminder that he could never have her. Never again call her his own. He had no business letting her touch him or wanting to return that touch.

She stood in her stocking feet, holding her brown pumps in delicate hands that still showed a fine tremor from the events she'd just seen.

But she wasn't looking at him as if he'd turned into a monster before her eyes. There was awe in her cinnamon eyes, a hint of residual fear—fear for him for standing in front of a car that would have flattened a lesser man.

And there was an emotion that looked like love in her eyes. It fired his memories, replayed his past. His past with this woman. And it hurt. God Almighty, it hurt.

He longed to tell her who he was, tell her the truth, open himself for all that powerful love to rain over him. But he wasn't the same man she'd loved a year ago. He was an oddity. A freak. Yet he couldn't stay away, couldn't stop himself from coming back for more, more of her sunshine, even though it caused him a sweet misery.

And it *was* torture, to want someone so desperately, knowing he could never allow himself to have her.

Darkness filled his secret heart. He felt as though he were trapped under a sheet of ice in a frozen pond, an experiment gone wrong sentencing him to a lifetime of loneliness.

Yet instead of leaving town as he should have, he'd stayed, selfish enough to want to take what he could get, a breath, a scent, a moment in her presence.

Steady, he cautioned himself, knowing his emotions were dangerously close to the surface, knowing it would hurt like hell when he had to let her go.

And he *would* have to let her go. She needed more, so much more than he could give. The clock was ticking on his life, the wear and tear of these strange powers reminding him he was living on borrowed time.

She was watching him, and for once he couldn't read her thoughts. Was she blocking him? Or was the leftover adrenaline causing an interference?

He didn't dare hope that this weird phenomenon was losing its strength, that somehow he'd wake up in the morning and, poof, he'd be normal.

"You've had a busy day," she commented.

"Yeah," he said dryly, feeling disgust. "Plenty of opportunities for superheroes."

She did touch him then, sneaked right past his self-pity, right past his defenses, sending his blood pressure right back up.

Her palm cupped his cheek, her soft gaze boring into his. The scent of vanilla curled around him, blocking out the smell of burned rubber.

"You're so hot," she whispered.

He tried to step back. She followed.

Her thoughts flashed right across his brain, amplified in bold, erotic color. Flowered sheets, whispers over heated skin, soft touches mapping naked bodies, worshiping . . . loving.

Her fantasies became his—*were* his. Heat exploded in his body, threatening his control, his unshakable vow.

His eyes narrowed as he reached up and snagged her wrist. "You need a social life, Miss Kincade."

"Are you offering, Mr. Walsh?" Her tongue made a sensual sweep over her pouty lips.

Adam ground his teeth, letting go of her hand. "What the hell are you trying to do to me?"

"I'm sure I don't know what you're talking about."

Again he tried to step away. And again she countered the move, as if they were doing an intricate tango.

Adam's fists clenched to keep from pulling her to him. "Better run, little girl. You're playing with fire. You don't want to get tangled up with someone like me."

"And what if I do?"

"Then I'd tell you that you weren't very smart."

"I've got a college degree that states otherwise."

"I wasn't talking academically."

"No. I didn't suspect you were. Can you honestly tell me you don't feel the magic when we touch?"

God, no. "You can't recapture your memories with me."

"Memories," she mused. "I do have plenty of those. I loved a man once. He told me he was in law enforcement. I never saw him at his job, never asked him to tell me about it. But I guess that's the thing about love."

Her eyes locked on to his, holding him in place. He couldn't have moved if his life—sorry as it was—depended on it.

"I learned something so powerful from that man," she continued softly. "I learned that love doesn't ask why, and it never explains . . . it doesn't think twice. It just surrounds you and speaks from the heart like a whisper from a distance." She placed her hand over her own heart, then touched the symbolic necklace, making the ache in Adam's gut grow.

"It's so complicated, and so very simple at the same time, and it doesn't always make sense." Her gentle gaze suggested there was an underlying meaning to her words, that to her, everything didn't have to make sense, that she wasn't a woman who looked at life in black and white.

That she was a woman who could—and *would*—accept a man with odd, unexplainable powers.

And Adam decided he was deluding himself. Big time.

"When our hearts make a choice, it's out of our hands," Molly said. "This man and I didn't have a lot of time together. He was on vacation and so was I. It was summer, so short, but so sweet . . . a magical summer."

Adam didn't know how much longer he could stand here and take her bittersweet account of her memories, her theories on love.

His jaw tightened. "Why are you telling me this?"

She shrugged. "I rarely talk about that part of my life. Maybe if I do, it'll put it to rest. Maybe I'll accidentally say the right word you're looking for, the word that'll convince you I just might be ready for someone else in my life." She gave him a shrewd glance. "That *is* what you said, wasn't it, Adam? One word and you'd take me up on what I was offering?"

"Cut it out, Molly. You're out of your league here."

"True. I've never put myself on the line like this, set myself up so blatantly for rejection."

"Damn it, I don't want to reject you."

"Then don't."

"I have to."

"Why? For my own good? What makes you think you know what's best for me?"

"I just do. Can't you leave it at that?"

"Oh dear, Adam," she said with mock concern. "I *am* making you uncomfortable. You're perspiring. Are you too warm in your sweatshirt?"

A burst of surprised laughter escaped him. "Damn it, woman. You're going to regret this conversation in the morning." Not only were her words making him sweat, but also he could feel the hum in his veins beginning to subside, feel the fluttering edge of weakness begin to invade. He fought it like mad.

"Well, no, I don't think so. I mean I wasn't exactly suggesting we strip here in the auto shop and go at it."

"So that's your angle. You're looking for someone to go to bed with?"

"Not somebody, Adam. That sounds crude. I'm looking for *you.*"

"Why?"

"Because I feel something. Something stronger than me. And I think you feel it, too."

"I'm attracted to you," he admitted slowly, reluctantly, feeling that much of a confession was safe.

"But you're afraid of me."

"I'm afraid of hurting you, yes. I'm afraid of you pinning your hopes on me being *him*. I'm not, Molly. I'm just not. And you're making it hard for me to be noble."

"Then don't."

"I'm going to pretend I didn't hear that."

"You're probably going to hear a lot more," she mumbled.

"Why?"

Her head snapped up, and she grinned. "Because I've decided it's unnerving the way you can read my mind. I figure if I just say what's there, it'll put us on more of an even ground."

"Forget it. I'll just make more of an effort to block you."

"Hasn't worked so far. What makes you think you can start now?"

"Because I can't let you go around blurting out improper suggestions."

"If it doesn't embarrass me, why should it embarrass you?"

"I didn't say it embarrassed me."

"Oh, then it must make you hot."

"Damn it!" he exploded.

And Molly burst out laughing. "Poor Adam. Let's change the subject."

"Gladly."

"Will you have dinner with me?"

Aw, hell. "Don't you have papers to grade or something?"

"Actually I do. I thought maybe I could get you to help."

"What do I know about grading papers? I'm just a guidance counselor."

"True. You know, you never did tell me what you did before you came to Clemons."

"No." He gritted his teeth. "I didn't."

She grinned. "Good thing I'm not one of those nosy types, huh? A really good example of that is the fact that I never pressed Jason to tell me about his work— or much about his past, for that matter."

"We were talking about grading papers," Adam reminded. He felt the approaching weakness, circling like a nebulous specter, waiting to pounce.

"Were we?"

"Yes."

"The essays I assigned, the one that Eddie did the show-and-tell on," she clarified, "turned out to be more lengthy than I'd anticipated. I thought since you were there that day, since you heard the passion in the students' voices over the state of the school system, you'd be a good judge of the papers."

When he didn't comment, she added, "As a counselor, it'd give you additional insights into their personalities. It's a great way to get your feet wet, Adam."

"My feet are feeling pretty soaked right now."

"Then might as well jump in all the way." Her eyes turned beseeching. "I really could use the help, Adam. I'm swamped. The kids were so enthusiastic about the project, it wouldn't be fair to make them wait for validation."

He'd never been able to hold out against Molly. He sighed, knowing when he was outmatched. He told himself he was strong, that he could head off this crazy idea of seduction she seemed to have in mind. And right now foremost in his mind was ending this conversation before he ended up in a heap at her feet. "All right."

"Thanks, Adam." She edged toward the door. "I'll meet you at your place, say, six-thirty? I'll spring for dinner."

She didn't wait for him to accept or reject. She just zipped out the door. Damn it. The woman operated at two speeds—full speed and warp speed.

But what the hell. If she was searching for clues to his life, she would find none at the mansion. Most of the stuff there belonged to somebody else.

Right down to the pictures on the wall.

The only reminder of their past together rested in his hip pocket, in a special fold of his wallet.

Chapter Eight

The neighborhood was so upscale, Molly expected to see movie stars cruising the streets in Mercedes-Benz and Rolls-Royce cars. She almost felt embarrassed driving her old, faded blue Honda down the palm-lined street.

She checked the numbers once more and pulled into the gated driveway of a sprawling house that had to have been built back in the 1800s. It could use a bit of a face lift, but it had character. Beautiful, exciting character.

She'd had to snoop in his personnel files to find the address. His application was downright sketchy, containing little more than a street address and a phone number.

Funny how she just now realized that she'd never been to Jason's house the summer they spent together, the summer they'd loved so completely.

Getting out of the car, she shook out the folds of her dress and took a deep breath. She'd dressed with care...to seduce. For that, she'd chosen feminine rather than vampy. The scoop neck showed just the right amount of cleavage and drew attention to her heart necklace. A rosebud print in soft yellows and blues, the fabric was incredibly soft and invited touch.

And she intended to invite Adam's touch at every opportunity.

Grabbing the pizza box and her satchel of papers to grade, she climbed the steps of the front porch and rang the bell.

He must have been watching for her. The door opened immediately.

And Molly simply stood there and stared. His navy pin-striped suit fit him to a tee, emphasizing his broad shoulders. A stark white shirt complemented his tanned skin and dark hair. The collar button was undone, his striped tie loosened, the knot pulled down, as if he'd changed his mind about the formality but had been caught before his decision could be reversed.

"You look—" she had to clear her throat "—very handsome."

He took the pizza box from her, unsmiling. There would be barriers to cross this night. His brooding expression told her so.

"You've seen me in a suit before."

"Yes. I just didn't expect it tonight. Here."

He turned and headed for the parlor. "I smelled like tire rubber. And I had an appointment."

With whom? she nearly asked. *Destiny? Me?*

The way he'd evaded her eyes told her he hadn't really had an appointment. She wondered if he'd worn the suit as armor. Jason hadn't worn suits. Did he hope that the clothes and the face would camouflage a connection so strong it fairly screamed?

If so, she'd be glad to tell him he was deluding himself.

He glanced back at her, and Molly reminded herself of her vow to speak her thoughts before he could read them.

"So, do we eat first, or do I get to take a tour of this great old house?"

"There's not much to see."

"Oh, come on. You might take possessions for granted, but this is a treat for me. I told you I've been dying to tour the homes in this area."

His eyes kept straying to her neckline, where the heart charm flirted with her boosted breasts. Wonderbras weren't just for small-busted women. They did incredible things for people like her who had generous proportions.

"Explore all you want," he finally said, dragging the knot of his tie down another inch.

Molly knew she was getting to him. So far, her plan was working well. She was here, in Adam's house. And he'd just given her permission to poke in the corners.

He hadn't been kidding when he'd said it was sparsely furnished. The foyer looked cavernous, with its flow of black-and-white marble squares, high ceiling and sweeping staircase curving upward. It was a fabulous old house with two kitchens and two wings of living quarters. She could picture teenagers living here, a place of safety. A haven from the violent storms of the streets and dysfunctional families.

It would need sturdier furniture, though. She glanced at the ladies' fainting couch visible through the parlor door, then at the chandelier above. First rule would be no sliding on the curving banisters or swinging from fixtures.

"I've just moved in," Adam said dryly, "and you're already ousting me in favor of teenagers?"

She laughed. "Sorry. I have a habit of being fanciful, of dreaming big. Someday I'd like to have a place like this, a refuge for my kids."

Adam watched her, enjoying her verve and her enthusiasm. He had a hard time keeping his mind off what she wore under that filmy dress and on the tour *she* was obviously conducting in *his* house. There was something different about her tonight, an air of steadiness that made him sweat.

"That's important to you, isn't it? Kids having a refuge."

"Yes. Everyone should have a place to go to where they feel safe."

"Did you?"

She shrugged. "Most of the time. My folks died when we were in high school." She stopped, turning to look at him. "You remember me telling you about my brother, Sam, don't you?"

It was a trap. Adam shook his head, hating himself for the implied fabrication.

"Oh, I thought I'd told you." She watched him, waiting for a reaction. He steeled himself against giving that reaction.

"Why don't you tell me about him now?"

She turned back around slowly, ascending two of the stairs, running a finger over the dust on the portrait of the old guy he'd dubbed "George."

"Do you know their names?"

She was referring to the portraits. Hell, was ESP contagious? And what happened to the brother stuff? Never mind that he knew all about Sam Kincade. Molly had raised him after her folks were killed in an accident, had battled to keep him off the streets and in school. A tall order for a fourteen-year-old girl. But she'd won. She might appear delicate and sweet, but Molly had a wealth of determination and a core of steel.

"I call that one George," he finally answered, then pointed to the remaining four photos. "That's Abe, Dwight, Ronnie and Waldo."

Her laughter swept the cavernous room, ricocheting off the walls and settling right in his heart.

"Waldo? How'd you come up with that one?"

Adam couldn't help the smile that tugged at his lips. Molly's shining eyes and sweet dimple invited company. "Look at that crazy haircut and tell me he doesn't look like a Waldo."

"Or an Alf," they both said at the same time.

Molly got so tickled she had to grip the banister to keep from falling. Adam's hand shot out, wrapping around her waist.

And in that instant, time stood still.

Molly felt her heart thump against her chest, felt her palms perspire, felt Adam's hands tremble at her waist. She gazed into his light brown eyes. So many secrets, she thought. So much pain.

He started to draw back, but she wouldn't let him. She cupped his cheek in her palm, her eyes begging him to stay. The word *love* flipped through her mind, over and over. Just the word. Nothing else.

"What?" His deep voice rasped along her skin, warming her and chilling her at the same time. "What do you love?"

Adam knew he shouldn't have voiced the question. Knew he should be running as far and as fast as his supercharged body would take him. Yet he couldn't move, was mesmerized by her voice, her scent, the feel of her tiny waist beneath the soft fabric of her dress.

"I love to teach," she whispered. "I love kids. I love to read and write in journals. I love to dance."

Her cinnamon eyes took on a faraway look, as if she'd forgotten he was here, forgotten she was telling him her innermost secrets.

"I love to make love...." Her sultry voice whipped through him, jolting him like a zap of 110 house current. "I love a man with a slow hand and an easy touch."

He groaned and her gaze sharpened, spearing him, holding him in a spell no amount of strength could break.

In that instant, he knew what her game was, knew she wasn't lost in thought after all. She knew exactly what she was saying and to whom.

And she knew exactly what it was doing to him. That much was obvious by the way she nestled into his hips, pressing, lightly, seductively.

"Slow and easy, Adam—" her tongue snaked out, wetting her full lips "—and hard and fast, all night, anytime, anywhere. I love to fantasize." A whisper now. So faint he almost didn't hear. "Please."

She'd pushed him to his limit. Never mind his good intentions. She'd drawn him in and she'd won. He could no longer hold out against her charm, needed a taste of her heaven, just once more, even though he was sentenced to a lifetime of hell.

The lure of temptation, of love, was just too damned much.

Slowly, hardly even aware of it, his fists unclenched. Knowing he shouldn't, unable to resist, he pressed her closer.

And she came willingly.

"Did I say the right word?"

"You damned well know you did."

"At last," she breathed against his lips.

He wasn't gentle, couldn't be gentle. Not after so long. He swept her up in his arms and took the stairs two at a time, his lips never breaking contact.

Everything he was, everything he'd ever be, would mean nothing if he couldn't be with her right this minute. She seduced him with a mere look, an innocent kiss, the sweetest, softest caress of her fingertips at the nape of his neck. Seduced him with her fantasies, her memories—*their* memories.

He couldn't allow himself to care about tomorrow, to hope, and God knew he'd given up on yesterday.

But he was scared. So damned scared.

His body hummed and his veins bulged. *Not now,* he begged, laying her gently on the bed. Never had he been so aware of a man's physical strength versus a woman's.

A tiny spitfire of a woman like his Molly.

He froze, his hand on his tie.

"Adam?"

"I don't want to hurt you."

"You won't." Molly held out her arms, her heart crying out at the agony she saw on his beautifully sculpted face, the agony of wanting something—her—so badly, yet for some reason being afraid to take, to give in to a desire that was stronger than both of them. "Kiss me, Adam. Start there. Just a kiss. The rest will follow. You'll see."

The clock on the nightstand ticked away the seconds as he stood there, indecision warring with invitation. At last he eased down on the bed beside her, holding his weight off her, resting in the circle of her arms—exactly where he belonged. His lips were warm and tender and erotic, an exquisite homecoming after too long of an absence.

She breathed in his sigh of surrender, her heart racing in anticipation. He wore no cologne, no artificial trace of scent to trigger memories. She might have told him that didn't make a difference. The connection was too strong, his natural essence a signature she would recognize anywhere.

Her blood pounded through her veins, building, needing to rush, yet his hands did no more than hold her gently when her body ached to be possessed.

She couldn't stand it, didn't want gentleness. Next time maybe, but not now. Something wild raced through her, a need so fierce she thought she'd break—an irrational fear that if she didn't rush, he'd disappear.

Her hands fisted in his hair, jerked at the knot of his tie, tore at the buttons of his shirt. She pulled him closer, closer still, until the pleasure bursting inside her bounded past reason.

Her urgency sparked a similar one in him. She heard her zipper rip, felt his muscles bunch, felt him go still.

"It's an old dress," she soothed, panting. "Please. Just hurry." In case he had any ideas otherwise, she initiated the action herself, dragging him along in her urgency.

Clothes were strewed across the bed, on the floor, discarded with little thought for fragile fabric.

And at last she felt him, all of him, skin to skin, burning her, healing her, making her heart sing.

She knew how his hands would feel, wanted to weep with the joy of that knowledge. So long, she thought.

He touched her with terrifying tenderness, as if afraid of his strength. She pressed him closer, soothing him, even though she thought she'd go mad.

"Let go, Adam. You can't hurt me."

"I could."

"Never. Unless you stop. Unless you leave me." *Again.*

The muscles in his arms bunched under her hands. He stared at her for a long, humming moment. In his eyes, she saw ribbons of color, the color of need and ecstasy and pain—the color of indecision and sweet resignation. And she saw the two of them, inside of each other, the shared memories, the endless nights of passion.

Eyes so blessedly familiar in a face so unfamiliar. The face of Adam Walsh . . . the eyes of Jason North.

Her hands mapped his shoulders, his chest, the swell of his firm hips, pressing, urging. He moved against her, his body guiding him even if his will balked.

"Yes," she whispered. "Make love with me, Adam."

The strain on his beautiful face was heartbreaking. She wanted to close her eyes against the pain, the emotion, but she didn't want to miss a single moment, a single hint.

On a tortured sigh, his lips once again closed over hers, and she welcomed him, reveling in that clever, sexy mouth, the taste she loved, the taste she remembered.

He caressed her breasts, his palms molding, worshiping, firing her senses, taking her out of herself, and when his tongue circled her nipple she nearly fainted.

Had it ever been this good? This strong?

Tormented, exhilarated, she tried to press him closer, but he evaded. She felt his warm breath at the inside of her thigh and nearly shot off the bed. Her breath sucked in, and her eyes did close then, colors bursting behind her eyelids.

He took her to heights she was sure she'd never reached. The power of his intimate kiss whipped through her. She sobbed out his name, writhing beneath him, frantic, shameless, praying for something, though at this moment, she didn't know what.

The climax slammed through her, incendiary, hard and shuddering.

She tugged at his shoulders, urging him back to her lips, pressing against him, needing more, so much more, her urgency making her greedy, undoing her.

"Let me touch you," she pleaded, surprised she even had breath enough to voice the words.

Adam didn't know how much more he could stand. Her sweet moans and frenzied movements had unleashed something wild in him, a force rushing through his veins that scared the hell out of him.

He tried to stop her, tried to get a firm grip on control, but she didn't give him the chance. She reversed their positions as if she were the one with superior strength, her hands and lips frantic in their trek over his body. He was burning up. Losing it. The single-minded attention she showered over his body hazed his vision, his mind. Her long silky hair trailed over his chest, his belly, his thighs. He gripped the sheets on the bed. Heard them rip. Felt her warm breath against the part of him that ached for release.

"Oh, please," he groaned. Those lips. Those full, sweet lips were both his bane and his salvation. The center of his fantasies, a sweet, erotic torture. Need built inside him. Hot-blooded and violent. His fingers fisted in her hair, gentled.

He pulled her up his body, beneath him, snatched open the bedside drawer and upended the damned thing. He stretched across her, reached for the floor, for the foil packet.

"You don't need—"

"Yes. I do." He couldn't take any chances of her getting pregnant, knew so little about the altered chemistry of his body—his DNA. A wave of loneliness and despair nearly brought him down. But his need was too powerful, his selfishness too great. Once more, he promised himself. Just once more.

She arched against him, her legs wrapping around him, her eyes closed on an emotion he couldn't read. He held on to his control by a thread.

"Look at me," he demanded, the words rasping past the thickness in his throat, the pounding of his heart.

Molly opened her eyes, searched the face that was so different, the scars that hadn't been there before— the one on his shoulder that *had* been. Felt the resolute, unmistakable connection of their hearts. "I love you," she whispered.

His eyes squeezed shut, shielding her. She gripped his hair, arched her hips, forcing his decision before he could deny her.

"I'm sorry," he said, his voice as harsh as his breathing.

She cried out in triumph as he drove into her, hard and deep. Like the final tumble of a combination lock, her heart opened, rejoiced, recognized and clung. Her blood pounded through her like hot lava, scorching her, chilling her, shooting her straight into a world of oblivion.

And when it was over, when she lay spent in his arms, their bodies still connected, still pulsating with a passion so hot, so beautiful . . . she wept.

"Oh, baby, don't," he said, his voice raw with emotion, with reverence, with sadness. "I don't know if I'll make it if you cry."

"I'm not," she said, her arms tightening around his shoulders, holding him fiercely, unable to let go. "I don't cry and I don't faint and I can stand up against any odds. The only way you can make me cry is if you leave me. Again." Her words were silly and made absolutely no sense in light of the wetness on her cheeks.

He didn't say anything. At least not with words. But Molly saw the truth in his eyes, saw the pain and hopelessness. She wanted to scream, to rage, to pound on him. He was already pulling back into himself.

"Why?" she asked. "Where have you been?"

The tears she claimed she wasn't crying spilled over her lashes, rolled into the damp hair at her temples, dripped over the skin of his thumbs.

He shook his head, prepared to deny.

She placed trembling fingers against his lips. "Don't. Not now. Not after this."

And in that moment, he knew he couldn't. Couldn't lie or evade. He'd caused her enough suffering— would cause her more. Not because he intended to, but because he had no control. He saw the plea in her eyes, the tenuous hope. God, he wanted to close the door and shut the world away until there was only him and Molly. But the world had a way of intruding, and time was so precious and short.

At last he nodded, all the fight gone from his wounded heart, prepared to answer and admit and let them both down as gently as possible. And that's the way he knew it had to be.

Because there was no hope. No *guaranteed* hope.

"What do I call you?" she whispered.

"Adam. Jason North is gone, half pint. There's a government death certificate to prove it."

Molly traced the scar at his brow, her emotions a riot of conflict. Pain—sharp and stinging—shot through her stomach, as did joy. The joy of rediscovery, of looking upon a face so completely different yet so lovingly familiar. The agony of an entire year, thinking he was gone from her. Forever.

And now he was here, in her arms. She felt a pang of anger over the deception, and just as quickly it died. He, too, had suffered.

"I have so many questions. I know I told you that love doesn't ask why, but I think in this instance I need to know."

He propped himself against the carved mahogany headboard, taking her with him, holding her against his side.

"I told you I was in law enforcement. That much was true. I worked for the FBI. The summer we spent together, I was on vacation. When I left you that day, I thought it'd be a routine day back at work. Nothing out of the ordinary. So when I was asked to transport a package to the main lab, I didn't think twice. And I didn't bother to ask what was in it. Do you remember that day?"

"Yes. September 10. It was raining. I remember thinking that September shouldn't be so gray and gloomy."

He nodded. "The rain kept up into the night. I started to call you, but I'd already told you I'd be gone for a few days. I was tired, and it was late. The windshield wipers could hardly keep up with the downpour. Then a dog darted out in my headlights. I was punchy, I guess. I yanked the wheel too hard, went into a spin, then overcorrected. My car hit a tree."

"Oh, Adam."

"The next thing I knew, a month had passed and I was in a government hospital. I was in a coma."

"So that explains it. I called all the hospitals in the area. They had no record of you. I fell apart, Adam. Each day it got worse. I couldn't work...I thought you'd been toying with me, that it was just a summer romance—"

"No, baby. Never that." His fingers, absently stroking her hair, stilled.

"But you let them tell me you were dead!"

She saw his jaw tighten, knew his reasons without him having to tell her—he'd called himself a freak. Later, she promised herself. Later she was going to slug this man. But not now. Not when she was holding him again after so long.

"What about your face?" She touched his cheek, his brow, wanting to kiss away the scars. "Why is it so different?"

"You don't want to know too many of those details. Let's just say there wasn't a lot to work with after the accident. Bone structure had to be rebuilt. This is what I ended up with."

"It's very nice. Beautiful."

He snorted.

"To me, it is," she said softly. "It confuses me, though. You feel like Jason. But you look like Adam."

"I *am* Adam. That was my middle name. I just dropped the first one."

"Why?"

"Because I wanted a new identity. I wanted out." His arm tightened around her shoulder. "I'd planned to resign even before the accident."

"I remember," she said softly. "And now you have."

"But not for the same reasons." For several moments, he didn't speak. Then his chest rose on an inhaled breath.

"They say I was clutching the package when they found me. There was a capsule in that package, an unidentified chemical. It didn't belong to the U.S., but they damned sure wanted to identify it, break it down."

"And did they?"

"No. When I left the hospital, there was still part of the formula missing. We've got great technology, but so far our lab boys haven't come up with the right combination."

"Is that what's changed you so?"

"That's a polite way of putting it, Molly. The stuff entered my system and made me a freak. Some sort of interaction took place when the substance came in contact with the metal pins in my shoulder."

"The injury you were healing from when we were together."

He nodded. "They've removed the metal, but it hasn't made a difference. Any time emotion zings me or my adrenaline pumps, something shifts inside of me. My fight-or-flight impulses have gone haywire. I guess I can be thankful that my clothes don't rip off or my skin doesn't turn green when it happens."

"Adam, for heaven's sake. It's not that bad. We can live with it."

He stiffened. "No."

She rose, propping her palm against his chest, curling her fingers into the mat of dark brown hair. "Don't you dare do this to me."

His jaw clenched. "I have no choice. This was a mistake. I shouldn't have let it happen. There is no future for us, Molly."

"How can you say that?" She wanted to hit him, but her arms felt paralyzed. "You loved me before. I know you did!"

"Damn it, Molly." He jerked away from her, putting distance between them, both emotional and physical. Naked, he rose from the bed and strode to the window. "I can't give you what you need. I can't give you a future."

His shoulders slumped. "I can't guarantee you I won't be dead tomorrow!"

Chapter Nine

Molly sucked in a breath on a wave of pain so strong she nearly doubled over. "But you said they were working on a cure! You can't be sure—"

"I've checked, Molly." His fists clenched at his sides. "I called the lab last week—for all the good it did me. The prognosis was worse than before. The adrenaline surges will eventually wear out my body. They're not offering me hope...or an estimate for life expectancy."

"No," she moaned, low and agonized, like a mortally wounded animal. She wrapped her arms around herself, holding on. "I've just found you again. I can't lose you!"

"Hell, I'm a bastard," he said, his voice sounding weary, so desperately alone. "Now do you see why this was such a mistake?" He gestured toward the rumpled sheets of the bed, still warm from their overheated bodies. "I was selfish. I took from you, revealed my identity, knowing I could give you nothing in return."

"But you can," she cried, rising from the bed, unselfconscious of her nudity. She needed to hold him, be held in return. "You can give me whatever time you have left. Don't you see, Adam? I never got to say goodbye before. I never had any closure. I couldn't hold your hand or touch your body or watch them lay you to rest. I could only torture myself with thoughts and images."

"And you think it'll be easier the next time around? Because you can *watch?*"

"Yes. That might sound morbid to you, but it's true. Don't deny us this time, Adam. I know about your gifts—"

He snorted. "Some *gifts.*"

She ignored his sarcastic interruption. "You only use your strength for a good cause. And just think of all the misunderstandings we can avoid with your ability to read my mind."

He frowned. "I'm not following your logic."

"That's just it. If you don't understand my logic, all you have to do is listen. Silently." She was fighting for her life. For *their* lives. She'd already faced the tears, more than her share of pain. The winds of her heart might have blown her down on occasion, but she'd gotten back up, stood her ground—just as she intended to do now.

They'd been given a second chance; she wouldn't let him run from her. She understood the loneliness she'd seen in his eyes, the solitariness. And the force of that understanding shook her.

She slid her hands up his chest, cupped his beautiful, somber face between her palms, saw his pupils dilate when she pressed her naked body to his. "Listen, Adam."

And he did, staring into her eyes. Just as she'd hoped, desperation and sadness slowly softened into reluctant amusement.

"Like *that,* half pint?" She felt his heartbeat pick up the rhythm of hers. "I'm shocked at you."

She smiled, the seductive smile of a siren, a siren who would go to any lengths to hold on to what was hers—to hold on to her love.

"Come back to bed, Adam, and I'll show you just how shameless I can be."

SHE WATCHED HIM SLEEP, afraid she'd never be able to close her eyes again, afraid to miss even a second of their life together.

He had the bravest of hearts, the strongest of souls. How could he even function with the loneliness that hung over him like a dark cloud? When he expected to lose everything—his life—at any moment?

No more, she vowed. Never again would this beautiful man face the night alone. Because now he was here with her. Maybe he hadn't intended it, but his heart had cried out to her, whispered her name. Not a shout—only a feeling. And because of that, because of her love, she would be there for him every step of the way, with every beat of her heart, with every breath that she took—whether it was a single day or a handful of years.

Somehow she would *will* him to live. They'd crossed the first hurdle. She'd reached out and he'd taken. And because of that courage, she would be his rock.

She snuggled down beside him, wrapping her arms around him as if she could absorb all his worry and pain into her. From now on, she'd risk anything, everything, body and soul, just to hold on all night, to never, ever let him go.

"WHAT HAPPENED to your heart?" Molly asked, touching the charm at her own neck. "The one that matches mine?" They'd finally decided to dress after a weekend of lovemaking. It was as if they were in a race against time. A race against a potential killer substance in Adam's body.

A race to cram a lifetime of living into uncertain, short days.

He zipped his jeans and reached for his wallet on the dresser. Opening it, he pulled out the symbolic charm.

"You have it," she whispered, her hands going still over the safety pin she'd used to repair the rip in her zipper.

"The chain was broken in the accident. I thought I'd lost this, too, but Frank had it."

"The man who called me?"

"Yeah."

"Was he your partner?"

"That and more. I was a kid pretty much like Lamar or Eddie, one of those kids who could have gone bad if somebody hadn't cared enough to step in and straighten me out. Frank did that for me. He cared. He became my legal guardian, my father and my friend."

Molly smiled softly. "I'd like to meet him someday." She saw his shoulders jerk and closed her eyes against the stubbornness in him she was determined to overcome.

"I'm starving," she said to distract them both. "Is there any food in this underfurnished castle?" So far, they'd been surviving on cold pizza, the pizza she'd brought with her Friday night and forgotten about until the next day.

"There's probably some eggs and stuff in the fridge, but why don't we go out? We could probably both do with some fresh air."

"Wore you out, did I?"

He stepped up behind her, easing the makeshift zipper into place, trailing his hands over her shoulders, his lips following, nipping at her neck. "Not likely, half pint. With you, I've got enough stamina for two men."

The instant he said the words, reality intruded. Hell, he had enough stamina for a hundred men. A stamina that could vanish just like that.

He met her cinnamon eyes in their reflection in the dresser mirror. As much as she wanted him to stay, he knew he'd have to leave her. She wanted to hold his hand in death. He didn't know if he could take that, to see the sorrow on her face. Somehow he had to get her to promise to get on with her life when he was no longer here.

Right now, with his hands resting on her silken skin, he couldn't abide the thought of another man touching her, another man basking in her laughter and sunshine. When his bones were turned to ashes, though, he wouldn't know.

He had no idea if death would come like a thief in the night or if he'd linger for months, perhaps years. But the thought of being weak and helpless, dependent on her compassion and loyalty as he lay wasting away, was intolerable.

Why couldn't they have given him answers? He'd spent the promised eleven months, being poked and prodded, performing like a circus animal. And it hadn't gotten him squat—other than a great deal of sympathy and respect for those innocent lab mice.

Still, he needed to make some plans, get his affairs in order—as Malcolm had gravely suggested. He didn't want Molly to watch him die.

So he would leave, just as soon as he knew she was taken care of.

His finger traced the broken zipper of her dress, the zipper he'd unintentionally ripped in a moment when he'd forgotten to temper his strength.

"Maybe we should stop by your place before we go out in public. This safety pin looks a little shaky. One deep breath, and it'll pop."

She smiled. "Is that your polite way of saying I'm falling out of my dress?"

"I love the way you fall out of your dress." His hands eased around to cup her breasts. The feel of her was sweet torture. Sure, he'd made up his mind to leave. But he still had time. And he was enough of a bastard, selfish enough to want to snatch every second of that time left.

"Don't start something you don't intend to finish, Adam," she warned, her brown eyes dilated, her lips moist and parted.

"You're right. Food first. Sex later."

She let her breath out slowly, and he grinned. Damn, he'd missed her.

As they started for the stairs, Molly paused, opening the closed door opposite his bedroom. He loved her innate curiosity, the way she made his head spin in her rush to experience every sensation, every new twist or turn, the way her sharp mind jumped from one thought to the next, planning, wondering, discarding, deciding.

This room was one that *did* hold some of his personal belongings. His weight-lifting equipment.

He saw her expressive eyebrows arch at the sight of the two-hundred-pound barbells that were curved rather than straight.

He shrugged. "Weight lifting was a part of my life that I used to enjoy."

"And you thought you needed to test your strength?"

"No. I thought it would relax me. But my mind wandered, and my thoughts went haywire. Next thing I knew, the damned things were bent like a pretzel."

Her sudden burst of laughter took him right out of his self-disgust and pumped his ego up faster than a shot of steroids. "What in the world were you thinking about, Adam?"

His eyes locked with hers. "You."

He heard the little hitch in her breath, saw her chest rise. Knew her thoughts as if she'd shouted them.

"Uh-uh," he said, shaking his head. "Even Superman needs to eat sometime. Let's get out of here."

"Well, if you're certain." She brushed by him, giving his biceps a quick squeeze, her cinnamon eyes sparkling. "Sexy as all get-out, if you ask me."

THEY DROVE up the coast with the T-top off the Porsche, to a little seaside café they'd been to before. The memories were as warm and faithful as the spring sunshine, washing over her, holding all the ugliness at bay. Here, by the sea, it was a different world, a world surrounded by swaying palms and the roar of the surf, of not-so-white sand and kamikaze sea gulls. It was a day for lovers to walk hand in hand or ride tandem on bicycles. A day to just *be*. To play.

"I want to deed the house over to you."

Molly's eyes rounded, stunned. "Why?"

"Because you were right. It'd make a perfect refuge for teens."

Butterflies took flight in her stomach at the thought of her dream being within grasp. At least, *one* of her dreams, she thought, the wings of excitement taking a dive. "But... why would the deed need to be in my name?"

"In case something happens to me. It's what I'd planned for all along, the reason I bought the place. To give it to you. The stipulation's in my will, but it'll make it easier on you if we do a title transfer ahead of time."

"Nothing's going to happen to you, Adam. You're invincible."

The words hung between them. A bravado that had no foundation.

"Molly—"

"Don't, Adam. Not today. It's too beautiful." She rose and held out her hand, noticing he'd already taken care of the breakfast bill and included a generous tip. "I want to kick my shoes off and walk barefoot in the surf. I don't get down this way too often."

He took her hand, his eyes telling her that reality would have to be faced soon, but that he'd give her today.

The shifting sand was warm beneath her feet. They had to pick their way around the bits of litter and broken glass. It was awful the way people had so little respect for the beaches, how they could, without thought, clutter up the beautiful, tranquil playground.

Grasping the sleeve of Adam's T-shirt, she skirted a jagged bottle, then shrieked with pure delight as he swooped her in his arms and jogged the last few yards to the surf. She wrapped her arms around his neck, her hair streaming over his arm, flying in the breeze. And she laughed—at the pure joy of being in Adam's arms, at the joy of spending the day with this man, in a setting she loved, in a place straight out of her own private fairy tales.

She buried her lips in his neck, inhaling his masculine scent.

I love you. The words trembled on her lips, but she left them unsaid. At one time, they would have tumbled easily and often, been accepted and returned. Now they would more than likely get in the way.

And today she wanted nothing to get in their way.

He knew her heart, and that was enough. Because right now they were on shaky ground. The despair still pulled him, threatening to take him from her. She'd seen it in his eyes when he'd talked about deeding the house to her. And she couldn't let that happen. She intended to hold him with all her might, be his strength, his salvation...his woman.

Be there when he reached for someone in the night, to chase away the nightmares and hold the uncertain future at bay.

"You can't take the whole world on your shoulders, half pint."

He set her down, the hard-packed sand now cool beneath her feet. Foamy surf swirled around her bare ankles, then ebbed out, sucking the foundation of sand from beneath her feet. She held on to Adam, determined to shore up *their* foundation.

"I can try. I might be little—"

"But you're mighty," he finished for her, his eyes telling her he shared her memories, cherished them, cherished her. "I don't deserve you."

"Yes, you do. Absolutely you do." She tugged at his hand, pulling him with her along the ocean's edge.

They walked in silence for a while, a comfortable silence, lulled by the roar of the surf and the excited cries of children building sand castles and darting to and fro.

"What do you hear from your brother, Sam?" Adam asked.

"Not much. And not often enough. You know he's a jet jockey now out of Miramar."

"A top gun, huh?"

"Yes, and has the cocky attitude to go with it."

"And you're proud as punch."

"Absolutely. Does it show?" She grinned up at him.

"Just a tad. You did good by him, half pint."

"Mmm." She accepted the admiration. "He did his part, too, though. He had the drive and determination to make something of himself. I'd saved enough of the life-insurance money from Mom and Dad to get him started in college. The U.S. government picked up the rest. Sam graduated at the head of his class. He claims he's a natural with the jets, that he's got the *touch.*"

"Doesn't surprise me. His sister's got a pretty great touch, too."

"Thank you for the compliment, but I think we're talking about two entirely different touches. You wouldn't get me in one of those screaming jets for any amount of money. There's something so thrilling about them, an excitement that just encompasses you when you watch them, but I'd just as soon have my feet firmly on the ground."

"You don't like to fly?"

"A commercial airliner might be fun. Safety in numbers and all that." She shrugged. "I'm not really sure, though. I've never been far enough from home to have a reason to fly." She gazed out over the ocean. "I've always thought Hawaii would be a great place to visit. Maybe we could—" She broke off, realizing what she'd said. She didn't want to shoot the easy mood between them. She knew they had to live each day as it came, that the future was so damned shaky.

Change the subject, she thought, her heart racing. *Quick.*

"Speaking of choices and young boys who make it out of the hood, what are we going to do about Lamar? He only made it to class two days out of five last week."

"We?" Adam asked, his brows raised in exaggerated astonishment. "You're actually including me in this?"

"Don't get cute." She bumped him with her hip and ended up setting herself off balance. Adam grabbed her before she landed in the surf.

"I could make a phone call. The INS frowns on sweatshops who don't even pay minimum wage. They'd shut it down in a heartbeat."

Molly frowned on that sort of thing, too. "Then do it."

"It'd mean Lamar would be out of a job."

"Yes, but he'd be in school."

"Maybe."

She glanced at Adam, wondering at his tone. "Do you know something I don't?"

"Hey, I'm *L* through *P*, remember? Castillo's your case."

She grinned. "Got to you when I told you I intended to watch over your shoulder, didn't it."

"As if you could even *see* over my shoulder, half pint."

She sent a spray of seawater in his direction, drenching them both. He laughed and hooked his arm around her waist, hauling her into his arms, protecting himself from another drenching.

Her feet were suspended off the ground, the fronts of their bodies pressed from chest to thigh. "Now how mighty are you?"

"I'd show you, but I'm too busy enjoying the feel of your hot body."

"Woman, you are shameless."

"You love it and you know it."

"Yeah. I do." His head lowered, his lips taking exactly what she offered so freely, so lovingly. She clung to him, wrapping her legs around his waist, uncaring that they were on a public beach with tourists and locals skirting them, surfers sitting on boards waiting to catch a wave.

Her hands cupped his beautiful face, and her fingers tunneled in his hair. She angled her head and took the kiss much further than either of them had anticipated. Their breaths mingled and tongues mated. Sunshine rained down on them, warming her body as love warmed her heart.

When it was necessary to come up for air, she still held him, with her hands and her legs and her eyes. The thrill of his touch trembled inside of her, shaking her right down to her bare toes.

Adam cleared his throat. "I like the way you play, lady."

"I wasn't playing," she whispered with what little breath she had left. "That was for keeps."

Longing, fierce and swift, flashed in her eyes, a longing he didn't think he deserved.

He let her slide down the front of his body, slowly, as if it pained him to do so. Molly took his hand, resuming their steps and their conversation as if there hadn't been a sensual hiatus, determined to keep any hint of sadness at bay. "What if we helped Lamar find something else? Another job with decent hours?"

"Might be tough to do on the up-and-up. He's only fourteen. Will the school issue a work permit?"

"Not till he's fifteen."

"Let me give it some thought," Adam said. And still, Molly got the strangest impression he knew more about Lamar than he was telling.

Chapter Ten

The hallways of his house didn't echo anymore, Adam realized. There were rugs on the floors and beds in the rooms. Heavy, depressing drapes had been yanked down and replaced by lace valances and fabric-lined shades. Molly had accomplished a hell of a lot in just two weeks.

The biggest change, the most noticeable to Adam, though, was his bedroom. Molly's perfume bottles now cluttered his dresser, and her clothes hung in his closet. She'd just bulldozed right over his protests and insinuated herself smack in the middle of his life.

"Just try and budge me," she'd said when he'd attempted to insert a measure of caution.

The fear of his body betraying him, going haywire and out of his control, scared the hell out of him. He hated living in limbo this way, sometimes wished that whatever was going to happen would just do it and be done with it.

But that would mean being without Molly. And he wasn't ready to give her up.

He shook his head and set aside his thoughts, picking his way around the tools left behind by the electricians and painters. The sprinkler company had been out to retrofit the east wing, which would house Molly's teens. Adam had people cutting through reams of red tape to speed up the certification process, and the attorneys were drawing up a new deed to transfer ownership from his name to Molly's.

She'd fallen right in with each process with her usual verve and whirlwind style—except for the last one. She didn't want clear title to the house. She'd told him that was negative thinking, that he was sticking himself in the grave before it was necessary, and she refused to even think about it.

But that was reality, and Adam needed to prepare for reality. He hadn't felt that odd hum of pain or the electromagnetic sensation as often lately, but he had felt the weakness. Without warning, it seemed to just hit him.

So far, he'd managed to hide it from Molly. He didn't know how much longer that would be possible.

He found her in the kitchen, hands on hips, her full lips pursed, staring at the commercial stove as if she expected it to spit out a gourmet meal like magic.

He grinned. Damn, she was special. "Looks plenty big to me," he said. "You gonna whip up a crowd-size batch of fried chicken, or what?"

She turned, her brows still drawn together. Every time he looked at her, his gut did a flip. He never knew what to expect and he loved it.

"Are you kidding? I'm the one who brings pizza, remember? This thing's got so many gadgets, it's scary."

"Can't feed teenagers a steady diet of pizza, half pint. Even though they probably wouldn't complain."

"I know." Her voice was so forlorn, he automatically went to her. She plopped down at the kitchen table and rested her forehead on her palm.

"What's wrong?" He squatted next to her chair, gave the braid that hung down her back a gentle tug.

"I've gotten so caught up in all of this, the excitement of remodeling, I mean. You can't imagine how fun it is to have free rein with somebody else's money—" She stopped, glancing at him with concern. "How are we doing budget-wise? I've tried to keep the costs down, but—"

"Don't worry about money. I had a sizable inheritance, remember?" *Jason North's.* "The government paid big bucks over their screwup. What else is bothering you?"

"I didn't think this through. Adam, I love my teaching job and I don't want to give it up. But the kids will need someone here. Who's going to run this place?"

He'd already had a few thoughts on that subject. "How about Eddie Martinez's mom. I did a little checking up on him—"

"Elena," she interrupted, reaching out to pat his cheek. "How perfect. I once tried to get her to go to a shelter, but she wouldn't. Said she wouldn't take charity. Her husband's abusive—it spills over onto Eddie. But I could pay her and . . ."

She jumped up and kissed Adam smack on the lips. Hard. And not nearly long enough. He reached for her, but she was already charging off in another direction. Hell, she was hard to keep up with.

"You're a genius!" She snatched up her purse and hooked it over her shoulder.

"Where are you going?"

"To see Elena Martinez."

"Molly, it's eight o'clock at night, for crying out loud."

"So?"

"So, wait for the sun, why don't you?"

"She'll be at work then. Best time to catch her would be now."

She rushed over and kissed him again, absently—on the cheek, damn it. Her mind was already tearing off in another direction, another cause.

"Seems to me we've had this discussion about the dangers of inner-city streets at night."

"Don't be silly. Elena Martinez walks those sidewalks every day."

Her logic confounded him. He took her chin between his fingers to get her attention. "Elena's not a shrimp schoolteacher with innocence written all over her pretty face."

"Oh, I do like compliments." She took his fingers from her chin and kissed them, too. "And because you called me pretty, I'll forgive you the shrimp part."

"Molly," he warned.

He could have saved his breath. She just tossed him a look and a wave and was out the door.

"Damn, I hate it when she does that," he muttered, and followed her out the door.

THEY WERE IN Molly's Honda, and he was driving. His knee jammed against the dash as he braked for a stray softball that rolled into the street. He swore, at the unthinking youngsters, at the thought of Molly traipsing around here on her own and at the throb in his banged knee.

Molly just tsked and glanced at him. "It's your own fault, Adam. I told you I'd drive."

"I'd prefer to make it there in one piece."

"Oh, you are so negative. But I forgive you." She patted his sore knee. "It's a man thing, I know."

He frowned, searching for a parking spot. "What is?"

"Your need to drive."

"Gender has nothing to do with it. I've seen you drive."

"You're pushing it," she warned. "First you call me shrimp—although you did temper it with a compliment—and now you attack my driving abilities. I'll have you know I've never been in an accident or gotten a ticket."

He rolled his eyes. "Thank God for small miracles. That's not to say you probably haven't *caused* a few accidents, the way you cross four lanes of traffic in one sweep."

"I have *not* caused any accidents. Anybody knows that timid drivers on a California freeway just get run over." She pointed to the curb in front of a fenced-in courtyard. "There's a spot right there. Pull in."

"That's not a spot, Molly."

"Of course it is."

"For a bicycle, maybe." He passed right by and hung a U-turn.

Molly bristled. *She* could have gotten the car to fit in there. "I should have insisted on driving," she muttered. "And I don't think I remember this bossy side of you. But hey, if you want to park two blocks away, that's your prerogative."

He didn't bother to level a comeback. In the end, he settled for a parking space only half a block away from the Martinez's apartment. It wasn't much bigger than the one she'd pointed out. *Men.*

"I heard that."

"I intended for you to."

They got out and walked the dark sidewalk. Adam wrapped his arm around Molly's waist, pulling her close to his side. She kissed his shoulder, letting him know she really did appreciate his protectiveness, even though she was perfectly capable of walking unaided.

The door to the Martinez apartment stood ajar, emitting a wonderful aroma of homemade tortillas and spices Molly wouldn't know the first thing about—other than that they made her mouth water. Frozen microwave stuff was more her speed. Canned laughter floated out from the sitcom showing on the small color TV.

"*Mihijo,* is there homework you should be studying?" she heard Elena say.

"You see, Adam?" Molly said, raising her hand to knock. "We have open doors, family hour on TV and caring parents. Now don't you feel silly for worrying so?"

He made a strangled sound deep in his throat, but Molly's knuckles had already rapped on the door-jamb. Eddie pulled the door all the way open.

"Hey, Miss Kincade. Mr. Walsh. Don't tell me I already blew the *A*. I only missed today. First day in a long time."

"Your *A*'s still safe, Eddie. That's not why we're here." She glanced past Eddie's shoulder and lowered her voice. "I need to talk to your mom about something. Your dad's not here, is he?"

"No." Eddie's chin jutted out. He had a smudge on his cheek that could have been dirt. Molly didn't want to speculate on it because it'd make her crazy. "Haven't seen him in a couple of days."

"Mihijo, who's at the door?"

"It's Miss Kincade. From school."

Elena came to the door, wiping her hands on an apron. She looked too thin and much older than her forty-five years. She gave Eddie a stern look. "Is there a problem with my son?"

"No, Mrs. Martinez. We're not here about Eddie. Well, not exactly."

"Come in. You know you are welcome in my home."

As long as her husband wasn't home. Molly could have finished the sentence that Elena was too proud to voice. "Thank you."

The rooms were small but well kept under the circumstances. Crocheted afghans and embroidered doilies hid the threadbare cushions of the couch. A leg on the table by the recliner chair had been glued recently, a sign that there had been trouble here.

It fired Molly's determination. Elena Martinez needed a refuge just as badly as some of the teenagers on the streets.

"Son," Elena said, "get our guests something to drink, and some of the tea cakes, too."

"No," Molly said. "Really, we're fine. Could we just sit and talk for a few minutes?"

Elena nodded and waited for Molly and Adam to sit before she perched nervously on the corner of a chair, her gaze darting to the door. Eddie stood by his mother's side, his hand on her shoulder. Molly knew they were both worried about Mr. Martinez showing up.

She felt Adam's thigh brush hers as he shifted on the couch. "Oh! I forgot to introduce you. This is Adam Walsh. He's a guidance counselor at the school, and . . ." She had to choose her words carefully. She wanted Elena and Eddie out of this dysfunctional environment, but she didn't want to wound Elena's pride.

"I've come to ask a favor." Unconsciously she linked her fingers with Adam's, drawing raised eyebrows from Eddie. "Adam and I are involved in starting up a halfway house for teens." She told them about Adam's mansion and his generosity in opening the extra wing for kids who needed a safe haven from the streets. Excitement over their plans sent her words tumbling out in a rush.

"But Adam and I both work during the day. I love teaching these kids and I don't want to give it up. But North Haven needs someone there full-time to run it."

Adam's head whipped around to Molly. He completely lost the thread of the conversation. North Haven? When had she named the place? And why had she used his former name? He watched her animation as she plowed right over any and all of Elena's objections. Molly's and his fingers were still linked together. Rather than let go, she used his arm, too, when she gestured to make a point. Up and down, in his lap, then in hers. He didn't think she even realized what she was doing.

But Eddie did. The kid had a speculative sparkle in his eyes and a grin on his face. He also had barely restrained hope on his young features.

"You don't have to answer now," Molly said. "You can if you want—I'd love it if you did. It would take such a load off my mind. But whatever you do, don't say no before you come out and take a look at the house. Oh, it's so wonderful. You'd have a whole section to yourself and...well, it's just too grand to do it justice with words. Please say you'll come have a look."

"It couldn't hurt, Mom," Eddie encouraged.

The longing on Elena's face, along with the indecision, was painful to witness.

"I don't take charity," Elena said, gathering her dignity even though her soft eyes said she wouldn't have a single qualm about leaving this apartment and never looking back.

"It's far from charity," Adam said, figuring he ought to contribute to the conversation. "If we don't hire you, we'll have to find somebody else. In addition to the living quarters, this is a paying position. And whoever takes it will earn every penny of their salary. Being a mother yourself, I'm sure you know how much work goes into caring for and feeding teens."

"Yes." Elena nodded thoughtfully. "And they need love. A no-nonsense mother who will bully them into doing their book work. And they must eat right." She was definitely warming to her subject. "I am a very good cook. You ask Eddie here. He will tell you."

Eddie nodded.

Adam stood, pulling Molly up with him. He handed Elena a card with their home phone number and address on it. "Why don't you sleep on our offer and call us tomorrow?"

"When will you be needing to fill this position?"

"We're ready whenever you are." That wasn't exactly so. Renovations were still under way, state certifications and local permits pending. He felt Molly's glance, felt the gentle squeeze she gave his arm in appreciation for his fib.

She stepped around him and hugged Elena. It always amazed him how easily her affections were bestowed, her way of making everyone feel special.

They made their way out the door, Molly once again slipping her hand in his with a naturalness that melted his soul.

"Miss Kincade?" Eddie had followed them onto the second-floor balcony. They stopped at the top of the stairs and turned back. The porch light glanced off his dark eyes, illuminating the sparkle of tears he tried to hide. "Uh . . ." His voice cracked. "Thanks. You too, Mr. Walsh."

Molly made a move toward Eddie, but Adam held her back. The kid was fighting for bravery. If she gathered him in her arms the way he knew she intended to do, Eddie would lose it. And tough-guy adolescents didn't deal well with embarrassment.

"It's a legit offer, Eddie," Adam said. "Make sure I see you in school tomorrow."

"Yeah, yeah." Eddie gave a macho wave and stepped back into the house.

"He could have used a hug," Molly griped, matching Adam's steps as they descended the stairs.

"Not with all these other guys hanging around outside. Come on, Miss Fairy Godmother. You've dispensed enough goodwill for one night."

She grinned up at him. "Oh, what a wonderful thing to say. I do feel a little like a fairy godmother."

"Well, tuck your wand away and let's get out of here before somebody steals the wheels off the car."

"Ah, so the real reason for leaving the Porsche at home comes out."

It gave him a punch in the gut when she referred to his house as home. "The tires cost more."

"Careful, Adam. I might start thinking you've developed an attachment for a possession." He noticed that she automatically went to the driver's side of the Honda.

"Wrong door, princess."

She shrugged. "Force of habit. I keep forgetting I now have a male ego to put up with."

He put a hand at her waist and urged her between the parallel-parked cars. She raised her brow at the lack of space between her Honda's front bumper and the rear taillights of the Chevy. It wasn't the same car that had been there before.

"Close quarters," she remarked. "Sure you don't want me to get us out of here?"

"No. I don't." He unlocked the passenger door, put his hand on top of her head and gave a friendly push.

Molly just grinned and reached for her seat belt. "Macho man." Her lips quirked and Adam's eyes narrowed. "Hey, I think it's kinda cute."

He just glared and slammed the door.

PROPPED IN BED, Adam watched as Molly came out of the bathroom, letting out a flow of steam and the scent of vanilla. It was like a fist in the solar plexus every time he caught sight of her. Her skin was pink from the hot bath, her face free of makeup. The thin, silky robe clung to her lithe body. He felt like the luckiest man in the world, knowing that in just a few minutes she'd be crawling into his bed, snuggling up next to him, her delicate fingers dancing over his skin.

But he wasn't the luckiest man in the world. In fact, he was probably the most unlucky. Because as much as he wanted to keep her, hold her to him right on into eternity, he couldn't.

He didn't have a future to give her. Couldn't guarantee her tomorrow, much less eternity. Still, these hours with her were his own slice of both heaven and hell. He'd take the one, selfishly, for just a little while longer, knowing he'd get the other soon enough.

"Molly?"

"Hmm?" She was bent at the waist, smoothing scented lotion over her legs.

"What was it that gave me away?"

She jerked, spilling the lotion, scooping it back into the bottle and carefully closing the cap.

Turning, she crossed the room and climbed onto the bed, crawling across the turned-back spread. He lifted his arm, making room for her against his side. Her skin smelled like every one of his fantasies, a signature scent he'd never been able to get out of his mind.

"I knew it was you. It had to be. Because when I fall in love, it's forever. And I found myself falling for you." She traced his face, the scar at his brow, the dimple in his chin and the scar there, too, reaching up to press her lips against it.

"And I could never forget your kiss." Her voice was hushed, as if to speak any louder might snap some invisible, fragile thread. "The last day I saw you, you kissed me goodbye. When you didn't come back, I kept remembering that kiss, the texture, the flavor, the style. I built dreams around it. I haven't kissed anyone since you."

Adam closed his eyes, knowing he didn't deserve this woman. He was a worthless ex-G-man who'd known nothing about softness until Molly had come into his world. She could teach him so much about life and love and loyalty. She had so much faith in him. If he only had the time...

"So when you kissed me at the charity dance, I knew, even though you denied it. It felt as if no time at all had passed." She scooted up his body and leaned over him, her heart-charm necklace dangling forward, tickling his bare chest.

Slowly her mouth lowered to his. He drank in her scent, unable to keep his hands off her.

"And I love the way you kiss me," she whispered. "The way you take my face between your hands, the way your fingers feel in my hair."

Molly used her tongue to trace the seam of his lips. "I'd know you anywhere, behind any face. Because I'm your lady, Adam." She wanted to say *love,* but held it back, never mind that he could read it in her thoughts, in her eyes.

"And you're my man. Sometimes it scares me, this power I feel, as if you're the other half of my soul. As long as I can hear the sound of your heartbeat, though, I can deal with the fear."

"Molly—"

She covered his lips, whispered into his mouth, "Don't think about tomorrow, Adam. Just give me right now."

Chapter Eleven

He couldn't fight her, was more than glad to take the coward's way out, to do as she asked and not think about tomorrow, to accept what she offered so freely. To give back in return.

He slipped the robe off her shoulders, reveling in the softness of her skin. *I'm your lady.*

This woman humbled him. She filled him with life when he considered himself half-dead. He was lost. And the more she opened to him, the deeper he fell.

"There were nights," he said quietly, holding her silky hair back from her face, "when I'd lay awake, sweating, so disgusted with what I'd become, feeling sorry for myself. And I'd dream about you. Just like this, lying above me, holding me." He felt her shudder of response, saw the desire dilate her pupils.

"Oh, Adam. I dreamed, too."

He tugged her face back down, angled her head and devoured her mouth, feeling frantic, as if alligators were snapping at his heels, as if he had to rush, to stay one step ahead.

He couldn't get close enough, knew he could never make it last long enough. He felt her pulse hammer beneath his fingertips, knew that the strength of this woman was a memory he would carry with him long past the grave. She never shied away from the power of his need. Instead, she matched it, gave it right back.

His hands swept over her, down her back. He cupped her buttocks, tilting her hips, pressing her against him. Her arm was still caught in the sleeve of her robe. She shook it off, impatience screaming, her body writhing against his.

Hot, so sweet. Her breasts crushed against his chest, her hips nestled into his, moving, restless, need building. He rolled with her, jerking her beneath him.

"No," she panted, pushing him back, wrestling him for the superior position. "Let me." She straddled his hips, her hands kneading his chest, his arms, all of him that she could reach.

Cherished. Her fingertips—so light, so erotic— danced over him, cherished him. Made him feel invincible when he knew the opposite was true. Emotion swelled in his chest, aching, threatening his composure. His throat closed. If he were capable of it, he might have cried. But he couldn't. He could only lie there, muscles straining, heart soaring.

He felt the familiar rush, tried to control it.

"Shh," she whispered. "Just feel. Easy."

Their roles were reversed. He should be calling the shots, yet it was she who gentled him. His Molly. So small . . . so strong.

Her lips trailed softly over his heated skin, nipping, soothing, exciting. She knew just when to press harder, just when a light touch was better. She found points of pleasure he hadn't known existed.

His hands skimmed her sides, tested the weight of her heavy breasts, circled and squeezed. Her skin was so delicate, milky white with a light tracing of blue veins just beneath the surface.

It was the hardest thing he'd ever done to lie there and let her minister to him, pleasure him. And when he could take it no more, he returned the favor, shifting her, using lips, hands, tongue and his whole body, gently, so gently, watching her, gauging her desire.

Molly felt the sting of tears. Something was different about his touch, a reverence that bordered on desperation, as if this would be their last time. But it wouldn't. The power of her love would make sure of it.

She felt the fever of his skin, held him tighter, willed him her strength, her love, her *faith*.

When his fingers dipped into her, her breath snagged. Like a match to dry tinder, her insides flamed, then swelled, throbbed. A white-hot flash of desire raced through her, leaving her gasping and dizzy.

The world spun away, narrowing to encompass just the king-size mattress and the two of them. And still he gave her no respite, no time to catch her breath. Her limbs felt both weighted and energized. He touched her as if she were the most precious thing, touched her as no other man could touch her. She could hardly believe such intensity existed.

Her body shuddered and clutched.

And when she felt his lips against her in the most intimate of kisses, she came apart. The instant climax rocked her. Colors exploded behind her eyelids, vibrant and erotic. The shudders went on and on. She gripped his shoulders, feeling both sluggish and empowered.

"Now," she begged. "Adam, now!"

She felt his weight shift, knew he was reaching for the ever-present condom. "No," she moaned, trying to tell him it wasn't necessary. She'd have his babies. *Wanted* his babies.

His eyes squeezed shut as he rose above her. "I can't chance it. You know that."

His voice was tortured. She knew he'd heard her thoughts. The thread of urgency waned as emotion twisted her insides into ropes of despair. "How long, Adam? How long before you'll chance it? A month? A year? Ten years?"

He covered her mouth, stopping her words, her plea. "I'm sorry."

"No," she whispered, realizing she'd allowed reality to intrude on their magic. He might not *have* a month or a year... or ten years. And that horrible threat made their time together all the more bittersweet and precious.

It was a time where there was no room for demands or decisions or dissension. Nor was it a time for tears or plans for a future. It was a time just to hold and be held tight in return, to live for the moment and make that moment the best it could be.

A time to build memories and dream.

So still. So utterly exquisite. His lips lowered, barely touching, breaths mingling, eyes wide open, holding, loving in utter silence, utter stillness. Like an ancient ritual that soon became an obsession.

Her heartbeat picked up in rhythm, thudding deep in her chest. She felt the sensations begin to build, like a ripple coming from a distant shore, gaining speed and momentum, a rush of power, of passion. Her chest heaved, the tips of her breasts touching his chest, retreating, pressing again with each inhale.

She shifted, urging him higher, silently letting him know it was time for more.

And he gave her more. Slowly at first, then with building speed, the friction of his thrusts taking her right to the peak of madness, then all the way over the top.

"ARE YOU GOING to get up some time today, sleepyhead?" Molly asked. Adam didn't budge and Molly frowned.

"Adam?" She touched his arm, felt the heat in his skin, the sweat at his forehead. Her heart trembled on the verge of panic. Heat was a good sign. It meant he was alive. But why didn't he wake up? He was normally a light sleeper; more often than not, he shot straight up if the bed wiggled.

She shook him, hard, her heart pounding in fear. "Adam!"

His eyes opened slowly, sluggishly. They were bloodshot, dazed.

She let out a relieved sigh. "Are you all right?"

He nodded but didn't speak. She pressed her lips against his temple, his eyelids, refusing to give in to the fear that tried to battle its way into her mind, conjuring all sorts of horrible scenarios.

"Sleep a while longer," she whispered. "I'll go make the coffee."

ADAM NEEDED DISTANCE. What he and Molly had shared last night had raked his soul, stunned him. He wanted to run from the pain, from something that was so right yet so wrong.

His eyes had finally opened this morning to greet the sun—after Molly had nearly pounded him. But would they tomorrow? He didn't know. The overwhelming tiredness scared the hell out of him. And because of that, he needed to tie up some loose ends. In a hurry. Before he became so weak—either physically or mentally—that she could talk him into staying.

He was sipping coffee when she came downstairs again, dressed for work in a pair of jeans and a tan blazer. Her heart-charm necklace flirted with the low-cut edge of her navy blue camisole. Looking at the jewelry, he felt blinded, felt as if his own heart had a crack in it.

Molly paused when she entered the kitchen, unhappy with the scowl she saw on Adam's face. Never one to shy away from unpleasantness, she breezed right up to him, slipped under his arm and stood on tiptoe to kiss him.

"You might as well stop scowling. If ESP's contagious, I think I've caught it. I can tell exactly what you're thinking."

"And what's that?"

"You've got one foot out the door, Adam Walsh, and I'll have none of it. So what if you were extra tired this morning. I get that way, too. There's no sense in even thinking about running away. I'll just follow."

"Molly..."

"Damn it, Adam! Just shut up, would you?" She actually astonished herself by stamping her foot. She *never* stamped her feet.

She'd obviously surprised him, too. His brows shot up, and his eyes widened. And true to form, Molly laughed. She braced a hand against his chest and rested her forehead there—and laughed. "Now see what you've made me do," she accused between gasping breaths. "My makeup's running down my face."

He tipped her chin up with his finger, his own lips quirked in a reluctant grin. "No streaks," he declared. "Fierce little thing, aren't you?"

She thumped him in the chest. "Watch it, buddy."

"I'd like to just watch you."

"Oh, what a thing to say five minutes before we have to leave for work." She glanced around the huge kitchen, then eased up against his body. The snaps of their jeans snagged. "On the other hand, that table looks about the right height. Care to call in sick?"

She felt his body's instant response, heard the deep growl in his throat. He hauled her in his arms and kissed her until she saw stars.

"Quick," she panted. "Hand me that phone."

"Uh-uh." His lips nibbled at her ear, sending chills racing down her spine.

"What do you mean, no?"

"Gotta go to work."

"Then what the heck are you doing kissing me like that and munching on my ear?"

He grinned. "Retaliation, Miss Molly, pure and simple. You make me hot, I return the favor. You had no intention of following through with that table suggestion."

"I do now."

"Sorry." He pressed a quick kiss to her forehead and set her away from him. "I'll take a rain check, though."

Oh, yes, she thought. She'd give him a rain check, all right. Because rain checks meant a person would be back, that they wouldn't run away.

"Think you're pretty smart, don't you?"

"I don't think it," she said with a grin. "I know it."

"Well, know yourself to work, would you?"

"Aren't you coming? I thought we could ride together. Same as always, ecology-minded souls that we are." When he stared at her with a strange frown, she clarified. "Car pooling, Adam. Less smog."

"Oh. I'm afraid we'll have to generate extra smog today. I've got to make a stop on the way."

"Where?" she demanded. He turned his back, rinsing his cup in the sink, taking more time than a simple rinse job warranted. She reached around him and twisted the tap. "Where?" she asked again.

His breath hissed out. "A certain sweatshop is scheduled to have a few uninvited guests."

"The INS?"

"Among others," he hedged.

"Then I'm going with you."

"No, you're not." He turned, pinned her with a narrow-eyed look. "You'll miss your first-period class."

"You've got a cell phone in the car. I'll get a sub for the class. Let's go."

He grabbed her arm as she headed toward the door. "This isn't something you want to get involved in, half pint."

"Who says I don't?"

"Me."

"Ah, my knight in tarnished armor." She patted his cheek. "You're sweet, Adam. But I'm a big girl."

"Damn it, Molly, you're not going."

She matched his scowl, unable and unwilling to back down. "You think Lamar's going to be there, don't you?"

He didn't answer, but his eyes betrayed him.

"Decide, Adam. Are we going together where you can keep your eagle eye on me, or do I take my own car? I know the way, you know."

He glared at her, shook his head, then stormed across the kitchen with all the grace of a charging bull.

Molly bit the inside of her cheek.

"Just once," he muttered, snatching his keys off a peg by the phone. "Just once I'd like to win an argument with you."

She laughed.

He shot her a look. "Go ahead and laugh now that you've gotten your way," he griped.

Molly saw the reluctant amusement in his eyes, the acceptance. "I like to get my way," she tossed back.

THE RAID WAS already under way by the time they got there. With the streets barricaded, they could get no closer than a block away.

Molly had the car door open before the Porsche had come to a complete stop.

Adam swore. "What are you trying to do—get your foot run over?"

She ignored him, her heart racing, her gaze scanning the milling crowd—curious bystanders speculating among themselves, hoping for a glimpse of danger, excitement.

"Excuse me." She pushed through the throng, aggravated that she couldn't see past the mass of looky-loos.

Adam grabbed her arm from behind. "Hold your horses, spitfire. They're not going to let you through."

"Well, don't you have a badge or something to flash?"

"Not anymore. I'm just a lowly guidance tech."

"Bull. You made the call. You can get through." She clutched at his T-shirt. "At least hoist me on your shoulders or something."

"I don't think that'll be necessary."

She followed the direction of his gaze. Lamar stood at the edge of the crowd, his fists clenched, looking like a scared ten-year-old rather than a teen with too many responsibilities.

Molly felt some of her tension ease. At least Lamar wasn't inside the factory, caught up in the confusion of explaining citizenship and proof of age.

She slipped her hand in Adam's and let him lead the way toward Lamar. His shoulders were broader. And the brooding, mysterious air that came over him when he single-mindedly focused on a goal made people automatically turn and step out of the way as if in a trance.

If she hadn't been so anxious to get to Lamar, she might have enjoyed standing off to the side to watch Adam in action.

Lamar was still staring at the signs being posted on the warehouse door: Closed.

He jumped when Adam tapped him on the shoulder.

"How come you're not in school?"

Lamar's frightened eyes focused first on Adam, then Molly, then back to Adam. "Don't like the hours."

"Oh, Lamar," Molly said. It wasn't like him to speak so belligerently. "Honey—" She reached for him, but he shrugged her off.

"Do you know what's happening here?"

"Looks like they're getting closed down," Adam said.

Lamar's face was set harder than granite as he stared at the commotion taking place a few yards away. He watched some of his co-workers being loaded into sheriff's wagons.

Slowly he turned, his eyes wild with a panic Molly didn't understand. Anger, she might have understood. Panic of this magnitude, she didn't.

"What have you done?" Lamar whispered harshly.

"It's for the best, kid. Places like this take advantage, paying less than minimum wage. It's not a good scene." He pulled a card out of his pocket with his home phone number on it, held it out. Lamar just stood there, frozen, his eyes unfocused. Adam stuffed the card in Lamar's shirt pocket.

The teenager jolted, came alive like a wounded dog who'd bite when in pain. "You did this," he accused, staring hard at Adam. "You've messed up everything! I needed that job. I need money! Don't you see, man? Don't you *see?* You said you were somebody I could trust, but you're not!" He let out a feral growl of helpless rage, spun on his heel and took off running.

"Lamar!" Molly started to give chase, but the steel band of Adam's arm around her waist hauled her up short.

"Let him go. He'll cool down, then we'll reason with him."

"Did you see the look on his face? Adam, it was the look of desperation."

Adam nodded. He'd seen it, and it made him edgy. "Seems we need to make a house call on Mr. and Mrs. Castillo."

LAMAR DIDN'T SHOW UP at school. Molly hadn't expected him to. During her free period, she tried calling his house but got no answer. To take her mind off the helpless look in Lamar's eyes, Molly settled on the old plaid couch in the teachers' lounge and pulled out a stack of papers to grade.

The door opened, and Adam walked in. He glanced at the coffeepot. "Ah, I see some resourceful person has made a fresh pot. Was that you, Miss Molly?"

"Do you see any severed fingers lying around?"

He chuckled and winked. "I love it when you talk tough."

"I better warn you I'm in a mood."

"Uh-oh. Should I put a warning sign on the door?"

She shrugged and set aside her papers. "Only if it says Privacy, Please. I need . . ." She turned beseeching eyes on him. "Could you just hold me?"

She saw him hesitate, felt her stomach twist. "Damn it, Adam," she snapped. "I'm fairly certain you're not going to keel over in the next three minutes. Just a simple human touch is all I—" Her hand slapped over her mouth. She felt her eyes brim. "Oh, damn, I'm sorry. That was nasty."

He eased down beside her on the sagging couch, gathered her into his arms. "Is this one of those days where everything's going wrong?"

"Yes, and I'm absolutely horrible for taking it out on you."

"Hey. I'm a pretty tough guy. Beat on me all you want."

"I don't want to beat on you, Adam," she said softly, turning her face into his chest.

He kissed the top of her head. "No, you just want to wave your fairy-godmother wand and cure the world of all its troubles."

"I'm going to send my wand back in for warranty repairs," she complained. "It's not working right."

"Oh, baby, it works right. But you can't save the whole world."

"I can try." She leaned back and looked at him, feeling the unstoppable current of love that passed through them each time their eyes met. "I can save you, too, Adam, from that dark place you keep going when you don't think I'm looking. I can make you happy. I can give you hope." She was grasping right now, jumping from one thought to the next. "Maybe they've found a cure—"

"Shh." He placed a finger over her lips, then replaced it with his mouth.

Molly clung to him, forgetting they were in the teachers' lounge, that anybody could walk in at any moment. She didn't care. She felt as though her lifeline was fraying. She didn't know why; she only knew that despair was pressing down on her, even though she tried to beat it back.

"Shh," he whispered again.

Dear heaven, she adored this man. She wanted to look forward to these strong arms waiting to hold her at the end of each day, yet knew it was way too dangerous to think past today, to think past right now.

Chapter Twelve

Elena Martinez stood on the porch, staring at the mansion in awe. Eddie had a similar expression on his face, but did his utmost to hide it behind the way-too-cool bob of his head under a set of earphones attached to a baby boom box.

Molly swung the door open wider. "Elena. I'm glad you could make it. Come in."

The woman wiped her feet on the mat and reverently stepped over the threshold. Eddie followed, his baby face splitting into a wide grin when Molly whipped the headphones off his ears. His shoulders never paused in their silent rhythm.

"Nice digs," he said.

Molly arched a brow. "Ah, a master at understatement." The foyer alone was bigger than what Eddie was used to living in. Bigger than Molly was used to, for that matter. She had to pinch herself every once in a while just to make sure she was really here—that it wasn't some fairy-tale dream.

"Let me give you a tour. Like I told you, this house is sort of split in two. To the right of this staircase is—" She almost said *her* and Adam's room. She wasn't sure how the staunch Catholic lady would take to that statement. Best to skirt it for now. ". . . where Adam's suites are," she continued. "To the left here—" she led the way "—is the east wing. There are eight bedrooms and four bathrooms." She saw Elena's eyes widen.

"I know. Sinful, isn't it? Sometimes I think I should be leaving a trail of bread crumbs or something. Anyway, the kitchen's a dream. You'll love it. The stove's a monster, but from what I've heard about your cooking, I know you're up to the challenge." She tossed a look over her shoulder, noticing Eddie poking behind every closed door they passed. Elena gave him a gentle swat, and he shrugged.

"It is a palace," Elena whispered.

"A messy palace at the moment. There are certain requirements to be met before we can legally open. I was hoping you'd agree to start early, to oversee the work going on."

Molly had a small jolt of reservation. Elena was timid and cowed by her abusive husband. How would she deal with male construction workers?

She saw Adam leaning against the counter in the kitchen. Alone, he wore a brooding expression on his face. He did that a lot when no one was around, when he let down his guard and didn't feel the need to present a front.

Molly watched Elena, wondering how the woman would react to his moodiness. After all, he was a virtual stranger who looked like he ate nails for breakfast.

But when she saw Elena bustle right into the kitchen, taking in all the fancy gadgets, she relaxed.

"Good morning, Mr. Walsh," Elena greeted. "Your North Haven is quite grand."

After only a slight jerk of his shoulders, Adam set down his coffee cup and pushed away from the counter, his features slipping right into the friendly-guidance-counselor persona, tucking the brooding scowl away as if it had been imagined.

"Mrs. Martinez. I'm glad you came."

"'Elena.' Please call me Elena."

Adam nodded. Eddie, who'd gotten sidetracked exploring, sauntered into the room, his lips pursed in a silent whistle.

"Hey, check out that table. Probably get twelve dudes around the thing."

"Eduardo, mind your manners," Elena admonished.

Molly had trouble following the exchange. She was too busy watching Adam, who was watching her in return. *Yes*, her eyes telegraphed. *You do owe me a rain check.*

The sensual images zinging back and forth between them were thick and powerful. And private. Heat crept up her neck as she realized what she was thinking about with a near-stranger and adolescent boy in the room.

Elena Martinez didn't appear to notice anything amiss. From the center of the room, she simply turned in a wide circle, taking in the grandness of a kitchen that alone was bigger than her entire apartment.

"Well, what do you think, Elena?" Adam said, dragging his gaze away from Molly's. Little spitfire didn't give his libido a moment's peace. "Is the position something you might be interested in?"

He heard Molly's smothered giggle, knew she'd automatically conjured up an entirely different *position* than he'd meant.

He sent her a sharp glance that said *I'll deal with you later.*

She sent it right back to him. *I'm counting on it.*

"Yes," Elena said softly, bringing focus to the confusion Molly could always create within him. "If the job is still open, I would like to take it."

Molly clapped her hands and beamed. "Excellent! Oh, Elena, you'll love it here. I promise. You too, Eddie." She raced over and hugged Elena, then turned to Eddie and treated him to the same affection.

She'd make a hell of a mother some day, he thought, and felt an instant, terrible punch straight to his gut.

Because he wouldn't be around to see it.

So he would continue his plans, plans to make sure Molly's future was secure.

"Elena," he asked quietly, "will there be trouble in your house because of this move?"

Embarrassment and fragile pride tightened Elena's too-thin face. For an instant, the only sounds in the cavernous room were the steady drip from the faucet the plumbers hadn't gotten around to fixing yet and the tinny beat of rap music from Eddie's headphones.

"Antonio has not been to the apartment this past week. When he comes back, I do not want to be there. He will not care. If I leave all of the things in the house as they are, he will be satisfied. His possessions are all that he cares about." She sent an apologetic look to her son. Eddie just shrugged, indicating he understood and had accepted the fact many years ago.

By damn, Adam intended to see to it that neither one of these fine individuals would ever again be used as a punching bag by a selfish drunkard.

"How soon can you be packed and ready to go?"

"There is not much to take. Tomorrow, I think."

"Tomorrow's fine. If Antonio shows up before then, you call me, understand?"

Elena nodded, and Eddie scooted closer to his mother's side. "Eddie," Adam warned as gently as he could, "if anything goes down, you just ride it out and let me handle it, okay?"

"Nothing will go down. We know how to not make him mad."

"Fine, then. I'll be by tomorrow with a truck to collect your belongings. In the meantime, just until the air clears a bit, it might be a good idea not to give out this address to anyone. I'll help you get started on the legal documents if a clean break is what you're aiming for."

"It is," Elena said, her voice stronger and firmer than Adam had heard so far.

Good. They didn't need irate ex-husbands making trouble in Molly's house of refuge.

The house of refuge she'd dubbed North Haven. He still hadn't gotten around to asking about that name.

AN HOUR AFTER Elena and Eddie left, Adam was still locked in a dark mood that Molly didn't understand. It worried her when he got this way. It usually meant he had one foot out the door.

"Think again, buster," she muttered.

"Did you say something?" He paused, paintbrush in hand. They'd decided to finish painting the kitchen themselves rather than wait for the contractor, who charged overtime on the weekends. Even though Adam had told her the extra charge wouldn't break him, it offended Molly's sense of frugality. She was handy with a paintbrush, she'd told him, and if *he* wasn't, it was time to learn.

"I said your face is going to get stuck in that position if you don't lighten up."

His scowl deepened. Obviously he was having trouble keeping up. Never mind her penchant for starting conversations in the middle of the subject. She always made perfect sense to herself.

"Seems a shame," she mused aloud, slapping a swipe of pearl white on the pantry wall. "Plastic surgeons go to all the trouble of making you look like a sexy movie star, and you mess up their work of art with frown lines."

She scooted by him, bumped him—on purpose—and gave the seat of his jeans a swipe with the dripping paintbrush.

He whipped around and stared at the sticky white streak on his butt. His forehead shot upward in astonishment.

Molly stuck her tongue in her cheek. "Oh, I beg your pardon. Did I get you with the paintbrush?"

Turning her back to him, she bit her lips to hold back a giggle, then shrieked when he grabbed her around the waist, spun her around and hoisted her over his shoulder.

The wet paintbrush slapped his behind again, this time purely by accident. "Adam!" She giggled, blood rushing to her head, the tip of her braid turning white where it stuck to the seat of his paint-covered jeans.

"We'll just see who begs whose pardon." He plopped her down on the tabletop, kicked the kitchen chair out of his way and wedged her thighs open, pressing against her in a way that made her laughter snag in her throat.

The dripping paintbrush clutched in her hands listed dangerously. Adam removed it from her fingers and laid it on a napkin.

"We're making a mess," she said, surprised she had the breath to do so.

"Yeah. And we're going to make a bigger one. It's not raining, princess."

His sexy voice thrilled her, shot her straight past preliminaries into full-blown desire. "Time to collect?"

"And then some." His fingers made short work of the buttons on her oversize work shirt, then gripped the waistband of her stretch pants. Bracing her arms on the table, she lifted just enough for him to jerk them off her legs.

The instant air touched her bare skin, she felt herself swell, ached for the touch of his fingers, his mouth, the feel of his hot skin. The button fly of his jeans pressed against her, causing a sweet friction, heightening her anticipation.

"One of us is overdressed," she panted, yanking the hem of his sweatshirt, leaving dots of white paint on his skin. She didn't want foreplay, was already hot and aching and ready.

Still, he tested her with bold fingers, driving her mad, taking her so high so swiftly she nearly screamed. She wanted him now, right here on the kitchen table, wild and unrestrained, hard and fast and deep.

Her heel caught on the rung of a chair, sent it crashing to the tile floor. She had a fleeting thought that he didn't have a condom with him in the kitchen.

She felt him stiffen and cursed her wayward thoughts. "Damn it, Adam. Don't you dare stop."

He hooked her legs around his waist, the material of his jeans rubbing against her naked skin, shooting her right to the edge of climax. She squeezed her legs around him, riding him as he strode out of the room and headed for the stairs.

"What about my rain check?"

"I'll still owe you—once I stock the kitchen drawers. In the meantime, there's a bathroom counter that's about the right height." The words were said around nibbles to her lips as his legs covered the distance between kitchen and bathroom in ground-eating strides.

Molly arched in his hold, teetering on the brink of a wild storm. The torrent washed over her before they ever made it up the stairs.

"NORTH HAVEN, MOLLY?"

She slipped a rubber band around the tip of her re-braided hair and glanced at his reflection in the bathroom mirror.

"Like it?"

He shrugged. "I hadn't thought much about it." Bull, he'd thought of little else since she'd dropped the name like an innocent lump of sugar at a polite tea party.

"Every refuge needs a special name," she said, turning to face him. "That one seemed to fit."

"But it's your place, half pint."

"I haven't signed the papers yet." She shot him a stubborn look. "I'm still not sure that I will."

"Molly—"

She plowed right over his objections. "If it hadn't been for Jason North, none of this would be possible. He was a hero, Adam. *Is* a hero." *The hero of my heart.* "North Haven will make sure he's never forgotten."

They rarely spoke about his former life, which was just as well. That person was gone. The face in the mirror confirmed it.

"There'll come a day when you'll have to let go, Molly. You've got your whole life ahead of you." And he didn't.

She hurled herself into his arms before he even had a chance to brace for her slight weight. Gaining his balance, he had no choice but to hold her.

"Don't talk like that, Adam."

"It has to be faced." The words scraped past the lump in his throat. They'd told him that each time his adrenaline surged, it would take another piece of him with it. Even something as natural as making love with Molly could very well trigger a reaction. "Sooner or later, it has to be faced."

Her fingers knotted at the back of his sweatshirt. She pressed her lips against his chest. "The paint's drying on the brushes. We ought to see to it."

"Evading the subject won't make it go away."

She leaned back in his arms, her cinnamon eyes reminding him of those of a small child who'd been told there was no tooth fairy. Accusing and hurt.

"If I have to face it, Adam, I will. I won't break. I'm made of stronger stuff than that. Until then, you can sleep in my arms," she said softly, "dream my dreams with me, enjoy each day as it comes."

Her voice gained strength and volume. "And if your faith is that shaky, then know this. I have more than enough for the both of us."

With each impassioned word, the knot in his gut coiled tighter. He reached around her and grasped the towel bar, bending the metal with an ease that suggested it was made of cotton instead of bronze. "Does this look like it'll go away on faith?" Disgust hung heavy in his voice. Heat burned like fire on his skin. He thrust his arm out toward her. "Does this?" He pressed the backs of his hot fingers to her cheek.

Her eyes glittered. "I know what's real, Adam. And I know what's right, what I feel deep down in my bones. If I have to face life without you some day, then so be it. But I don't *feel* it." She placed her hand over her heart, her fingers trembling. "I don't feel it here." Her fist closed around her charm necklace. "I've always felt the connection, like a fire in my soul, nudging my subconscious. And I was right. You're here. I'm touching you, talking to you, making love with you. So don't you dare discount my faith."

"Molly..."

"No." She jerked out of his arms. "I'm going downstairs to clean the paintbrushes."

He caught her wrist, snatched her back into his arms, buried his face in her vanilla-scented hair. And held on, his insides trembling. He'd never been a man to pray. He did so now, prayed with every ounce of conviction in his sorry soul, prayed even though he never expected to be granted the one thing he'd give anything to possess.

Molly. In his future.

ADAM RENTED A PICKUP from the local U-Haul company to collect Elena and Eddie. Their belongings didn't even begin to fill the bed of the truck.

"Don't really matter," Eddie said when he saw Adam staring at the empty space that could have hauled much more. "My mother doesn't need reminders of the man she married. And you said we didn't need no furniture at North Haven."

It still gave Adam a punch every time the name was spoken. And it bothered him that this fourteen-year-old kid felt he had to be so brave.

"Eddie, drinking changes people, makes them do bad stuff. Don't let anger eat at you. Maybe some day your dad'll get some help."

"He ain't my real dad."

Ah, hell. "Sorry."

"Yeah. Me, too. I remember my real dad. He worked for Southern California Edison." Eddie said the name of the utility company proudly. "Drove a company truck and all. I was just a little kid, but I can still see him. Antonio took all my pictures, but I painted one in secret, from my memories." He glanced at his duffel bag. "I hid it, and I still have it. Just a piece of paper, but it looks like him."

"So what happened to your real dad?"

"Transformer blew up. Killed him." His dark eyes fixed on the apartment he'd just been in for the last time. "Antonio took advantage of mom's sadness. Went through her money, then turned mean."

Adam reached out and squeezed Eddie's shoulder. "He won't touch her again, Eddie. You'll be safe with Miss Kincade."

"Yeah, man. I'm not worried. I could take the old fart if I wanted to."

Ah, the bravado of a fourteen-year-old. "I doubt that'll be necessary. Come on, kid. Let's get your mom and get out of here. And Eddie?"

"Yeah?"

"I'll buy you a picture frame."

Eddie ducked his head and slipped his headphones over his ears. And Adam pretended he hadn't seen the sheen of tears in the kid's eyes.

"OH, MY," MOLLY SAID. "I think I've died and gone to heaven. The smells coming out of this kitchen are wonderful!"

Elena wiped her hands on her apron, grabbed an oven mitt and opened the monstrous oven. "Enchiladas, my own recipe. They will be ready in no time. You kids go wash up.''

Molly chuckled and glanced at Adam. They'd just been called kids. All her reservations about Elena being able to handle unruly teens dissolved. Adam, Molly and Eddie nearly mowed one another down on their way to the sink, no one even thinking to disobey the order.

''Hat and stereo off at the table,'' Elena said to Eddie.

Adam shared a look of commiseration with the boy. ''Got you coming and going, don't they, kid? Miss Kincade at school, Mother at home. You won't be able to win for losing.''

''It ain't so bad—''

''Isn't,'' both Molly and Elena said.

Adam rolled his eyes, and Eddie cracked up laughing.

Damn it, this felt good, he thought. He shouldn't let the easiness lull him, but he was tired of fighting it. Everybody deserved a little time off for good behavior, he told himself.

Not that his behavior was all that good. Selfishness was not an admirable trait.

Still, just for a while.

He whipped a tea towel off the rack and dried his hand. When the phone rang, he didn't bother to reach for it. Molly was closer.

He saw her smile slip, saw her knuckles turn white against the receiver. ''Lizzy, slow down, honey. I can't understand you. Stop crying now." She paused. "Yes, Mr. Walsh is here. You have a card with his name on it?"

Adam was at her side, his knees bent, his ear pressed next to hers. She held the phone out slightly so he could hear the little girl's frantic voice.

"Lamar's gonna get in trouble. Said he's gotta make money. He's meeting some guys. You gotta stop him."

Adam straightened and reached for the Porsche keys on the peg by the phone. The keys bit into his palm as he waited for her to hang up. "Where?" he asked.

Molly was already headed for the door.

"What's happening?" Eddie asked.

"Lamar's in trouble. I've got to get to him."

"You're not going, princess, so you might as well slow down."

"The hell I'm not."

"Damn it, Molly—"

"You're wasting time and breath, Adam. I've got the information and I've got my own car. Now, are you coming or not?"

He swore.

And Eddie slipped right past him.

Hell, let's make it a party, he thought. He snatched Eddie by the back of the shirt. "Don't even think about it, kid."

"These are my people. I know how these things go down."

So do I, he thought, *better than you think.* The image of Lamar's gun upstairs in the bedside drawer flashed in his mind. "There won't be room in the car, Eddie. Stay here by the phone. We'll call."

It'd be tough enough just keeping an eye on Molly.

Chapter Thirteen

Adam shut off the engine and coasted in with the headlights off. Good thing there wasn't the loss of power steering to worry about. But even if there had been, the way his emotions were screaming right now, he could have twirled the wheel with a single finger.

They were half a block away from the rendezvous point Lizzy had directed them to. Thank God Lamar'd had enough sense to give Lizzy their phone number. He just wished the kid had exercised similar good sense and stayed home where he belonged.

"This is my fault," Molly said. "I shouldn't have encouraged you to tell on the garment factory."

"None of that kind of talk, Molly. How long do you think the kid would have put up with those chintzy wages? This was inevitable."

"It *shouldn't* be inevitable!"

"Life's tough." He scanned their immediate surroundings as he opened the car door. "Just push it closed," he said. "Don't slam it."

"But then it won't lock."

He spared her a quick glance—one that didn't need clarification.

"Oh, right. Just a possession."

The industrial park was dark and deserted. Adam didn't like the feel of it. "I don't suppose you've had a change of heart and will stay in the car?"

"Not a chance."

"That's what I was afraid of. At least stay behind me."

She touched his cheek, ran her finger over the dimple in his chin, the scar there. "Don't be a hero, Adam."

"Isn't that just what I am?"

"Damn it, you're strong, but a bullet can still cut you down."

"Then I'll make it a point to stay out of the way. Which is all the more reason for you to do as I say. You break my concentration, and we're in for it."

"Oh, good, put a guilt trip on me."

Their bickering stopped abruptly as a shot rang out. "The decision's out of your hands now, Molly." He reached under his sweatshirt and palmed his weapon, an action that was second nature to him.

"You have a gun!" she stated unnecessarily.

"Get back in the car and call the cops!" He didn't wait to see if she complied. He took off at a run.

He went in low, his back to the graffiti-covered wall, the .38 pistol high and ready. Footsteps pounded against concrete—three or four suspects, he calculated. Sweat beaded his temples, stung his eyes, yet his hands were rock steady.

A careful, darting glance around the corner told him the situation. One down. One standing over the body. An exit to the east—an alley. The layout focused in his mind like a perfect blueprint.

One step and a pivot, and he had his gun trained on a stunned teen.

"Drop it, buddy."

The kid stood in indecision, his eyes wild with panic above the bandanna that covered his nose and mouth. Great. Modern-day bandit. He didn't dare take his eyes off the kid to check Lamar.

He stared at the thug's eyes, letting his subconscious absorb posture and reflex: arm at a forty-five-degree angle. Gun unsteady—thinking about it. Buddies had already split.

So who was this creep? Adam wondered. The shooter? Or one of the pack with a conscience?

"Don't even think about it, kid." His voice, low and deadly calm, barely disturbed the night air.

"You a cop?"

"Nope. And that makes me your worst nightmare."

More indecision. *Hurry up!* his mind screamed, while his body remained steady, relaxed even. Lamar was moving. A good sign. But he was losing blood. Not a good sign.

Adam took a step, then another. Closing the gap. The gun shook in the bandit's hand. The kid was new at this.

"Better decide quick. This .38 has been known to have a mind of its own. Goes off all by itself sometimes." He shrugged nonchalantly. "I hate it when it does that. So messy, you know?"

He saw the kid hesitate, then bend slowly and set the weapon on the ground. "Smart move. Kick it out of the way." All the while he kept moving closer. The gun went sliding across asphalt. A .45. Hell, the kid didn't even realize he had Adam outgunned.

"What's the next move, man? I ain't armed no more."

"Funny," Adam said. "I've been asked that pardon-or-punishment question three times in as many weeks. I'm tired of being a good guy. Your loss."

Like the strike of a snake, his arm whipped out. Before the kid even had time to yelp, Adam had him tossed into the metal Dumpster at the back of the alley. He slammed the lid down and bent the metal, creating an impromptu prison.

"That'll hold you till the cops get here." The Dumpster had plenty of air inside—stinky air, but it was better than the little gangster deserved.

"Man!" the kid shouted, banging on the metal. "A bullet's got your name on it for sure. Ain't nothin' you can do about it, man. Wait and see!"

"That bullet's going to have to stand in line," Adam muttered. His own faulty body chemistry had first dibs on his life.

He turned back to Lamar just as Molly rounded the corner. She came to an abrupt halt and slapped a hand over her mouth. Shock registered in her wide eyes as she stared at the pool of blood under Lamar's shoulder.

Adam swore. He didn't know which one to take care of first. Lamar or Molly. In the end, he didn't need to make a decision at all. Molly's core of steel kicked in.

She ran to Lamar and bent over him, her soft voice asking questions and answering those same questions before Lamar could decide if he had breath enough to speak.

Adam whipped his sweatshirt over his head, tucked the .38 in the waistband of his jeans and knelt on the other side of Lamar.

"Did you call for backup?"

"Yes. I hear the sirens now. I told them to send an ambulance, too."

"Good thinking." He ripped his sweatshirt in half and packed both the front and back of Lamar's wound. "How you doing, kid?"

"Hurts. Not too bad, though."

"It'll be sore, I'll give you that. Looks like a clean entry and exit wound. A little disinfectant and a stitch or two, and you'll be tossing hoops in no time."

"I was stupid," Lamar said, tears leaking out of the corners of his eyes.

"Of course you were," Molly said so sensibly that Adam almost smiled. She used the hem of her shirt to wipe away the boy's tears. "Now, don't talk. The male of the species talks entirely too much if you ask me."

Adam raised a brow. Man alive, this woman was something. "I don't recall anybody asking for that particular opinion. Have a heart, Miss Molly. We've got a shoulder wound here."

"Yes, I can see that. And silence makes you smarter, if you know what I mean, Adam."

"Absolutely. And since smarts is your business, I'll defer to your superiority."

He kept one hand on the makeshift pressure bandage on Lamar's shoulder and put the other on Molly's back. Her muscles were rigid. She was holding on by a thread and itching to hit something. He knew her well. Thus her request for silence. If you gave this woman enough time, she'd sift through her feelings, hold on to the good, discard the bad and get a grip.

The quickest way to make her lose that grip was to talk.

Lamar appeared to have forgotten his wound. His interested gaze volleyed back and forth between Molly and Adam.

The siren whoops became louder. The strobe of red and blue announced the cavalry before the vehicles actually came into view.

And that's when Adam remembered the .38 shoved into his waistband—in plain view since he'd used his shirt for first aid.

"Uh, Molly? I know you've requested silence, but we've got a problem."

"And that is?"

"My weapon. Adam Walsh isn't on the government records."

She understood the situation immediately. He had friends in high places who could get him out of a jam, but it might mean several hours in lockup until it got straightened out. Jason North had carried an FBI shield. Adam Walsh was simply a guidance counselor at Clemons High.

She pulled up the back of her shirt. "Stick it in here. The things I do for you," she griped.

"Damn it, Molly. Where the hell's your purse?"

"In your unlocked car announcing its availability."

After a brief wrestle with indecision, he shoved the weapon in the back of her jeans and snatched the hem of her shirt over it just as a couple of LAPD black-and-whites screeched to a halt, high-powered spotlights glaring. The officers crouched behind open car doors, weapons drawn.

"We've got a shoulder wound," Adam called. "Not life threatening, but he needs an ambulance. One perp's in the Dumpster over there, the others got away—probably a ten-minute lead." He nodded to the .45 Colt several feet away.

"Kid in the Dumpster dropped that."

Molly glanced at Adam. "How did a kid get in the Dumpster?"

"I put him there."

"Oh. Why isn't he getting out?"

Adam shrugged, looking at Lamar and the police officer, who both appeared highly interested in that answer. "When I flipped the metal lid over, the damn thing bent in on itself."

"Oh, dear," Molly said, "wasn't that a lucky thing?"

Having gotten the all-clear from the police, the paramedics rolled in with a stretcher. Adam stood, drawing Molly with him. "Let's give them some room to work."

"Miss Kincade?" Lamar said, his voice shaking with fear.

"I'm right here, sweetie."

"Don't leave, okay? I gotta talk to you."

"I won't leave. But I believe we've already covered the subject of talking. Hush now and let the paramedics have a look at you."

She turned to Adam. "I'll ride in with him. You can follow in the car."

"I'd have suggested just that." He gave her braid a gentle tug and pressed his lips against her temple. She might boss and sass, but he felt the tremor of anxiety that ran through her compact body. "You going to be all right?"

She nodded. "I'll be fine. I'd be a lot finer if these damn kids wouldn't go around shooting one another."

"That's my Molly. Determined to save the world."

"Maybe not the world, Adam, just those who are mine." She gave his bare shoulder an absent kiss, then jumped as if something had goosed her. Her eyes rounded. *I've got a damned Smith and Wesson poking me in the butt!*

He leaned down, whispered in her ear. "Safety's on. Chamber's empty. Clip's in my pocket. Your butt's perfectly safe."

"Thank you," she said. "I think."

He waited until she climbed in the back of the ambulance with Lamar, then headed for his car. A slip of paper was anchored under his wiper. His eyes narrowed as he got a good look at it.

A parking ticket.

He'd gotten a damned parking ticket! His chest tightened, and his blood boiled. For crying out loud, a kid had just been shot, drugs were sold on street corners like candy, guns hawked like yesterday's newspapers and he gets a damned parking ticket! On a deserted street. He wasn't blocking any driveways, and no fire zones were posted.

He stepped back and slammed into something solid, automatically reaching for his weapon before he remembered he'd disassembled it and given it to Molly.

Heart pumping, he turned slowly. A parking meter. Emotions all over the place, he gave the thing a shove. It bent into the shape of a giant U-turn sign, pointing straight to hell.

Great. In addition to parking fines, he could be facing destruction-of-city property charges.

MOLLY HELD Lamar's hand as the ambulance sped through the city streets. They didn't bother with sirens, since his condition was stable.

"Miss Kincade, you gotta see about Lizzy."

"I will, honey. How about your mom? Does she work nights?"

Lamar's eyes darted away. "My mom's gone."

"Gone? Where?"

"Dead."

"Oh, honey. When?"

"'Bout eight months ago. It's just me and Lizzy now. She'll be scared. You gotta see about her."

The knot in Molly's stomach grew even tighter. Dear God, these kids were living on their own. Legally she ought to report it to the authorities. They were underage. But she'd done the same thing—when she was exactly Lamar's age. She'd raised her younger brother on her own and lied to the school system, afraid if they found out they'd separate her and Sam. The same thing could very well happen to Lamar and Lizzy.

And Molly knew she couldn't do it. This boy had been through too much. Damn, why did the world have to be so tough for kids?

"Miss Kincade?"

She squeezed Lamar's hand. "I'll take care of Lizzy. You just worry about getting better so you can get back in school."

Through the back doors of the ambulance, she saw the lights of the city, people walking on sidewalks, friends gathered on street corners. It all looked so innocent, yet could turn deadly in an instant.

Molly wanted to scream at the senseless injustice. She truly believed that education was the key. If these kids would fill their minds with knowledge, learn a trade, embrace a goal, their self-esteem would strengthen. They'd work toward a better life, a life where they could live proudly. Safely.

She looked back at Lamar's young face, at the white gauze wrapped around his shoulder. No. She wasn't going to turn this kid in. She was going to *take* him in. He had a mind like a thirsty sponge. If given half a chance, he'd make something of himself.

She intended to see that he got that chance.

ADAM WAITED by the emergency-room doors, watching as the ambulance backed in. He'd raced like a demon to get here first—parking-meter assaults aside. He didn't want Molly facing this situation on her own.

Hell, every time he thought things were squared away, that he could start to ease back, all hell broke loose, tossing him right back into the thick of her life.

He felt his emotions ebb, impatiently wiped the sweat from his brow with the back of his arm. His knees threatened to buckle, so he leaned against the wall, praying that his strength would last. He couldn't remember when he'd felt so damned tired. Hell, if he wasn't careful, he could easily slip right down this drab wall, end up in a heap on the floor. They could haul him in right next to Lamar and all the other patients.

And wouldn't the doctors have a field day with the results of his blood tests, he thought in disgust.

He noticed the relief on Molly's face when she saw him waiting. He hated that bruised look in her eyes, her guilt because she couldn't fix an entire world, a world that would take a hell of a lot more manpower to fix than just a half-pint teacher who had a core of steel beneath the sweet exterior.

He could use a little of that steel right now himself.

She eased up next to him, slipped her hand into his as they wheeled Lamar through the emergency doors.

"Adam, you're trembling. Are you okay?"

"I'm fine."

She studied him, pressed the backs of her fingertips to his cheek. "Your skin's burning up."

"Don't fuss, Molly." This was exactly what he'd hoped to avoid.

Her eyes narrowed. "It wouldn't kill you to lean on me, you know."

"No, my freaky blood's doing an adequate job of murder all by itself."

"I'm sorry. I lost my head," she whispered. "I understand." He wouldn't chance creating a child when the substance that altered his body chemistry was still unidentified. And still unspoken was the awful reality that he wouldn't leave her to raise a child alone.

She wrapped her arms around his shoulders, held on, absorbed him right into her soul, apologized with the sketch of her lips against his sweat-dampened shoulder, against the scar where the metal pins had been removed.

Where before there had been urgency, now there was quiet solace. And when at last he eased into her, it was a restful coming-home, a rightness that bolstered and rejuvenated and rejoiced. So easy, so silently, with gazes locked and hearts whispering. With no second thoughts, no explanations, no past or future. Just now. Two souls merging, a moment out of time.

Love doesn't ask why, she told him again, using only her body and mind, not her words. *It speaks from the heart and never explains.*

She felt him swell even more inside her, felt his acceptance, his appreciation . . . his love. So they took what they'd found in one another, that once-in-a-lifetime bond, and allowed it to wrap around them, fill them—accepted the celebration and joy and tenderness of the moment.

No words.

Their bodies spoke, softly, slowly, faithfully. A beautiful joining that transcended the physical. He was buried deep inside her, and she felt him throb, felt her own response, synchronizing as their two hearts became one.

"If you didn't look like you were about to fall over, I'd hit you for that."

His lips twitched. If there was such a thing as being healed by faith, his Molly could do it. She simply refused to believe the worst—about anything.

"Fine. Be a macho man. I need your car keys," she said.

He handed them to her without thought, then wanted to snatch them back. His brows flattened. "Where are you going?"

"To get Lizzy. Lamar's been raising that little girl on his own."

"Which explains the unreturned phone calls by the Castillos. Look, why don't you let me—?"

"Don't start, Adam. There's a scared ten-year-old worried about her brother and alone. I'm going to pick her up, and you're going to stay here with Lamar."

He took a mental step back, felt like grinning but was seriously concerned that she *would* clobber him. "Yes, ma'am."

She nodded, her eyes narrowed, her features tight. "And Adam? You'd better push those certification people. Paperwork or not, these kids are coming home with us." She kissed his cheek and absently patted his chest in a gesture so loving it was all he could do not to slump back against the wall again.

Adam watched her walk out the doors, her spine stiff, her stride filled with purpose. God help anybody who had the misfortune to get in her way. He had an idea he might need to buy another house.

North Haven would violate the occupancy limit within a week the way Molly collected strays.

Slowly, putting one foot in front of the other, he made it past the ER nurse by telling her he was Lamar's guardian. The kid looked young and scared lying in the curtained cubicle. Hell, he *was* young and scared.

"How's it going, kid?"

Lamar shrugged and winced when the action pulled at the bandage on his shoulder. "Did Miss Kincade go for Lizzy?"

"Yeah. She'll be back before they're even ready to spring you, so don't worry." He pulled up a chair and prepared to sit. His left knee gave out, and he sat. Hard.

He heard Lamar's worry and shrugged. "Old injury," he explained even though he hadn't been asked. "What happened tonight?"

"I needed money. I used the last of what I had to get the electricity turned back on."

Hell, these kids had been living in the dark.

"Some guys were putting pressure on me to join up with them. I thought it was the only way, easy money, you know?"

"Drugs?"

"Yeah, man. But I got scared, tried to back out. And when I did that, they thought I was a snitch." He crooked his uninjured arm over his eyes. "They wanted me to take a territory that I just couldn't. I'd have to hit on the kids Lizzy's age—over at the elementary school. I couldn't do it, man."

"Why not?" Adam snapped, then made an effort to temper his tone. "Drugs are drugs. What does it matter whether it's a ten-year-old or a sixteen-year-old? It'll still mess up a life." God, how he knew that. He had a chemical in his system, and it wasn't something he'd intentionally taken. Still, it was ruining his life—whatever it was.

Lamar winced and brought his arm down, his voice choked. "It wasn't just Lizzy that made me back out. I did it for Miss Kincade. She's always harping on choices. Telling us we can be *more*. I *want* to be more."

Chalk one up for Molly, he thought, wishing she were here to hear this, to know that she *had* made a difference. A spitfire who didn't take any guff from anybody, yet had a heart as big as an ocean.

He'd thought she needed somebody to watch over her. But she didn't. She did just fine on her own. *She* was the one with the strength.

Now he knew with a certainty that made him ache that it was time to pull back. To ease out of Molly's life before she was forced to witness more trauma— before the borrowed time he was living on exploded in their faces.

She might be strong, but he'd be damned if he'd hang around and let her watch him die.

Chapter Fourteen

Lamar recuperated nicely under Elena's clucking and Molly's no-nonsense caring. Lizzy, who'd been dubbed kitchen assistant, was in her element. Cookies shaped like Mickey Mouse heads and plates of brownies lined the granite countertops; threatening everyone's waistline.

The lawyers were squared away, deed and title-transfer papers already signed by Adam—still sitting *unsigned* by Molly. Every time he handed her a pen, she simply turned her back on him and claimed writer's cramp from grading papers.

When the time came, though, when her hand was forced, it would be a simple formality.

And that time might be sooner than he expected. Adam hadn't regained his strength after the last incident with Lamar. Hell, he couldn't even lift a two-hundred-pound barbell—a weight that had been a cinch even before he'd acquired these freaky powers.

Feeling as if he were eighty instead of thirty-five, Adam made his way through the den. He heard

Molly's voice, heard her talking to someone in the foyer. A man.

His gut jolted with both excitement and dread.

"So you're the Frank Branigan I've heard so much about. I'm happy to meet you at last."

Adam stopped, his sneakers rooted to the tile floor. Frank Branigan's gray eyes were tilted at the corners, eyes that could—under certain circumstances—turn cold and deadly like the flick of a light switch.

Right now, though, as his ex-partner gazed at Molly, there was nothing lethal about the look. It was friendly, intrigued and way too speculative as far as Adam was concerned.

At fifty-eight, Frank was in better shape than most men half his age. The evidence showed in the way his knit shirt banded his biceps and clung to his rock-hard stomach.

Snow white hair against a tanned face and a lady killer smile were things Adam had teased the man about. Now he didn't feel like teasing, didn't like the way Frank's eyes were clinging to Molly as if she were the best thing since sliced bread.

Which she was. And Adam was a fool to feel threatened by this man. His friend. His surrogate father.

As if Molly felt his presence, she turned, held out her hand. "Look who's here, Adam."

"I can see." He took her outstretched hand without thought, held his right one out to Frank. "You slumming, or what?"

Frank accepted the handshake, then went one better and pulled Adam to him in an embrace that had gentled a hard-nosed teen so many years ago. An embrace that made his throat ache.

"I'd hardly call this place slumming. Since I've been enlisted to use my considerable weight and persuasion this past month, I thought I'd come out and see what all the hoopla was about."

"So *you're* the mover and shaker," Molly said. "And all along, I've been giving Adam the credit." She cut her gaze to Adam, then stood on tiptoe and brushed her lips against Frank's cheek. "Thank you. You G-men are handy to have around."

"Hey," Adam said, "I made the phone calls."

She laughed and treated him to a similar kiss. "You two go plant yourselves and catch up. I'll make coffee."

Adam watched her leave the room, noticed that Frank, too, did the same, a besotted look on his face.

"She knows?" Frank asked.

"Yeah." Adam led the way into the parlor. The room had Molly's stamp all over it. Easy chairs with movable ottomans, bookshelves with everything from Byron to Stephen King, lacy drapes to let in the light. A refuge that invited you to put your feet up and stay awhile. "She guessed. I should have known. I should have been out of here sooner. I blew it."

"Don't be griping now, son. You made the choice. You came back here."

"I didn't think she'd recognize me."

"So you just wanted to practice a little masochism, that it?"

"Hell, Frank, what was I supposed to do? She was smack in the middle of four thugs with a switchblade at her throat!"

"You were always an exceptional agent. Never once blew your cover."

"I didn't want to blow it this time."

Frank pinned Adam with a look that took him back twenty years, to an interrogation room that had started his life on an uphill journey of discovery. A look that shamed and bullied and cared. A look that said there was always a choice.

"Yes, you did," Frank said quietly. "That little gal gave you hope. A damned good thing to have. There's no shame in it. Now I'm here to offer you more."

"More what?" Molly asked, carrying a silver tray laden with cups and a slender carafe into the room.

Frank shot Adam a questioning look.

Adam shrugged, his eyes clinging to Molly. His Molly. Frank had taught him he always had a choice. With Molly, he was afraid he didn't.

"Might as well spill it. If we try to keep secrets, she'll get ticked. It's a scary sight."

"Darned right it is," Molly said. "What are you offering our Superman?"

"A chance at being a weakling again."

The cups rattled on the tray, betraying her emotion, yet her expression never changed.

Adam frowned, pretended affront, pretended Frank hadn't just dropped an offer that would grant every one of his damned dreams. "I've *never* been a weakling." Except for that emasculating bout with the weights.

"Dump the ego," Molly said, setting the tray on the coffee table, her eyes never budging from Frank. "How?"

Adam growled, "I *am* in the room, you know."

"Sorry," she said absently. "You're excused. How, Frank?"

Frank chuckled. "I like your lady, Jas—Adam."

"Yeah. I like her, too." He reached for a cup of coffee, figuring he might as well excuse himself for all the attention either one paid him. "The sassy mouth's questionable, though."

"He likes my mouth, too."

Hot coffee spewed clear across the table as Adam choked.

Molly gave his back a gentle thump and grinned, never missed a beat. "Well, you do."

His narrowed gaze focused on her lips, those full, sweet, *talented* lips. Hell, she made him hard with just a look. Did she have to add her erotic thoughts to the mix?

"Charming," Frank mused aloud. "Absolutely charming."

"Can we get to the point?" Adam grated.

"Malcolm wants to do more tests."

Molly's coffee sloshed over the rim of her cup. Adam didn't move so much as a muscle. He felt frozen, shell-shocked, as if a grenade had just exploded in the room instead of six innocent words. Time was marked by the click of the grandfather-clock pendulum. Three beats. Four.

"What kind of tests?"

"He's made headway, possibly developed an anti-dote."

"Is it dangerous?" Molly whispered.

Frank shrugged, the tick at the corner of his mouth giving away his tension. "What's not dangerous now-adays?"

"What are his odds?" Molly insisted.

"Fifty-fifty."

She slid right into the chair beside Adam, her fingers gripping his, uncaring that the chair was only designed to fit one person.

"You'll have to do better than that, Frank. Is that fifty on the optimistic side, or are you a pessimist like Adam?"

"I'm afraid I do share that trait with him. In my gut, though, I want to lean toward optimism. I have to."

"And if it ends up on the minus side of the scale . . . will it mean he'll just go on as he is now?"

Frank looked away, fists clenched against his thigh. "No. It'll either work or . . . it could kill him."

The deadly slash of a switchblade couldn't have ripped her flesh as excruciatingly as those stark words. Her heart pounded, and her insides twisted in a mass of violent trembling. *Not yet,* she wanted to scream. *I can't lose him yet.*

She turned to Adam, cupped the side of his beauti-ful face, felt the fever he hadn't been able to shake, stared into the eyes she loved so much. *Don't do it! Please! Just stay here with me.*

"I'll do it," he said to Frank, his tortured eyes never leaving Molly's. "It's for the best, half pint."

"Is it?" The scream built inside her, louder, deafening, a buzz that threatened to turn her world black. She battled it back with every ounce of her control. She had to be strong. For Adam. She had to have hope. Frank had said *could*.

Adam nodded. "There's no choice. It'll kill me anyway if we just leave it alone. You've seen how I've been the past two days. It's better this way. Better to have closure."

She wrapped her arms around him, held him so tight there was little space to breathe. Frank slipped out of the room, the sight too raw to watch.

"When do we leave?" she whispered.

His shoulders went rigid under her hands. "You can't go with me, Molly."

When she drew back, fire burned in her eyes. She opened her mouth, but he placed a finger there.

"You have classes to teach. You can't leave those kids."

"Yes, I can."

"No. You can't. What about Lamar and Lizzy? Eddie and Elena? Your dreams are here, with the halfway house."

"My dreams don't mean anything without you."

"Shh." He kissed her eyelids, cupped her face and tunneled his fingers in her hair. "What happened to the lady who had enough faith for both of us? The one who swore she could face anything?"

"She's on vacation."

He smiled, surprised he still could. "Better call her back on duty. There's a lot of needy teens out there who are counting on somebody to offer them refuge."

She buried her face in his neck again, her breath hitching. "Not yet, Adam," she whispered, her cheeks wet with tears. "One more day."

"Molly—"

She covered his lips with hers, the salt of her tears tasting of both hope and despair, burning their way to his soul.

"I need one more day to find my feet. So I can kiss you without these wimpy tears."

He shouldn't agree. Should leave now. Make it easier on both of them. Instead, he swept his thumbs gently beneath her eyes and nodded. "One more day, half pint."

HIS DUFFEL BAG WAS PACKED and ready just inside the parlor door. He'd tied up as many loose ends as he could.

Frank came down the stairs, his tanned features drawn. "Sure you don't want me to go with you, son?"

Adam shook his head. "Somebody's got to watch over Molly. You've got the time coming. It means a lot to me...knowing she won't be alone."

"I'll stay."

Adam looked around the room, feeling as if he was forgetting something, feeling empty. His gaze rested on the portraits hanging on the staircase wall.

"Frank?"

"Yeah, buddy."

"If it doesn't work, you make sure they toss this worthless carcass in a furnace somewhere. I don't want anybody crying over my grave." Not that there was a whole line of people who'd actually care enough to do such a thing. But Frank might.

And Molly would.

"If that's what you want, I'll see to it."

Adam nodded and dragged his gaze from the lonely portraits. Molly came across the foyer, a small jeweler's box in her hands.

"I'll just go see what Elena's cooking up in the kitchen," Frank said, excusing himself. His hand rested on Adam's shoulder for a brief instant, gave a squeeze. Then he pursed his lips and whistled a jaunty tune as he crossed the foyer and disappeared down the hallway leading to the kitchen.

"All packed?" Molly asked.

"Yeah. Did you sign the papers?"

She glared at him. "No."

"Molly—"

"There's an error on them."

"What error? I've gone over them myself."

"My last name's spelled incorrectly."

"No, it's not."

"It is if you agree to marry me."

He closed his eyes, holding on to his control. "Molly, please sign the damned papers."

"I will when you get back. When the correction's been made."

God, she was stubborn. And brave. And strong. And he'd give anything to have her as his wife, to hold on to her forever, to never let go.

"I might not come back, Molly. You know that."

"You have to! Promise me, Adam. No matter what. You've *got* to come back!"

Don't make me go through the hell I did last time.

Her tortured thoughts singed him, made him weak. He didn't remember his mother, had never known his father. Few of the foster families he'd lived with had ever given a damn. The only people who'd really cared about him were Frank and Molly. There'd never been anyone in his life who'd hold his hand when he was sick, cared as Molly did.

She humbled him. Made him bleed. "What if I can't?"

Her back went ramrod straight, her eyes shooting darts of steely determination. He was in for it now.

"You can and you will. I either see you walk through this door or somebody calls me so I can go to you. I don't give a fig about top-secret facilities and hush-hush stuff—you tell them that!" She gripped his arms, shook him to make her point, the flat jeweler's box thumping him lightly on the jaw.

He'd forgotten the word *can't* wasn't in her vocabulary.

"You're not going to die on me, Adam. If you do, I swear I'll kill you."

Regardless of the grave situation, Adam found that he could still laugh. "My little spitfire. What's in the box?"

She took a deep breath, gathered her emotions like a cloak and popped the lid of the velvet box. A gold chain spilled out into her fingers. A gold chain that matched hers.

The other half of her heart charm hung from the end. Adam automatically touched his hip pocket where his wallet rested.

"I don't usually go through a man's things." Her eyes were filled with a caution he hadn't seen before. "Will you wear it for me?" she asked softly.

He was almost afraid to reach for the offering, afraid it would burn him.

"You haven't said it, Adam. I feel it every time you touch me, but I need the words. Please say you love me."

"Molly...everything's so uncertain."

"All the more reason. Don't make me beg—" her eyes widened "—unless..."

He snatched her to him, holding her, pressing her head against his shoulder. "No, baby. You're not wrong. I do love you. More than life. I don't want to hurt you again—if I don't come back..."

"You will come back," she whispered fiercely. "And I'll be right here, Adam. Waiting."

He closed his eyes on a wave of despair, a wave of uncertainty he couldn't control.

"I know you're breaking up inside, Adam. Don't give in. Believe in me. In *us.*"

She unclasped the chain, hooked it around his neck, rested gentle fingers against the charm. If the power of her love had wings, he was sure he could have flown. She gave him strength when he was so damned weak, using only the feather-light touch of her fingertips. He'd hoped to spare her pain, had wanted to take care of her, keep her safe.

Instead, it was she who gave the care and promised safety.

"You are my light in the dark, Molly Kincade. You say everything so right. I grew up never knowing there was anybody who cared—who *could* care so deeply. Frank came close, but you . . ." He couldn't go on.

He kissed her, letting his body speak when he no longer could. He kissed her without reservation, fiercely, his hands circling her face, their restraint underscored by the tendons that stood taunt on his forearms.

It was a kiss that said everything he could not, that spoke of hope and fear and love. A kiss that had the power to shut the world away, for just a while.

Until the blare of a taxi horn intruded.

Without speaking, they drew apart. Her fingertips traced his features, gently, lovingly, as if she were reading his essence in braille, committing every pore into memory.

He stepped back, lifted his duffel bag. She touched four fingers to her lips, transferred them to his.

As she'd promised, her eyes were dry when she kissed him goodbye.

His weren't.

"Come back to me, Adam. Come back and sleep in my arms."

Chapter Fifteen

The days ran into one another, becoming a blur. But Molly kept busy, kept up hope—most of the time. The nights were the worst, the times when her arms felt so empty, when her heart ached with loneliness.

It took every ounce of her willpower not to beg Frank to call the government hospital to get a progress report, even though she suspected he'd already done just that. He wasn't saying anything, though, and Molly kept the wings of panic at bay, hid her fears behind a smile that felt forced.

As she came downstairs, the happy sounds of teenagers who teased, bickered and laughed flowed out of the den. It was a sound that warmed her soul—the sound of her dreams.

A dream that would be complete if only Adam would come back to her.

Her steps slowed on the staircase, and she paused below the portraits of George, Abe, Dwight, Ronnie and Waldo, her fingers tightening around the five-by-seven photo in her hands.

"Dinner!" Elena bellowed, giving Molly a jolt. She smiled at her own jumpiness. The changes in Elena Martinez were many, and she had an idea Frank Branigan had a lot to do with them. The two had become quite cozy since his arrival.

Lamar, Lizzy and Eddie barreled out of the den, where they'd been annihilating one another in a Super Nintendo game that Molly still couldn't get the hang of.

"Eddie?"

All three youngsters skidded to a halt, their sneakers squeaking on the tile floor. Elena and Frank came out of the kitchen to see what the delay was, and stopped when they saw Molly standing on the stairs.

"Yeah, teach?"

"I need a favor, and you're just the guy to provide it."

Eddie smirked and nudged Lamar in a good-natured gesture that teased yet didn't compete. "Hear that? I'm into passin' out favors."

"Yeah," Lamar said. "Like you're so good at it."

"You heard her. I'm the man." He thumbed his chest and bobbed his shoulders and neck to the ever-present rhythm that played in his head. "Whatcha need, Miss Kincade? Fix your grades? Wash your car? Set VanArk's nose hairs on fire?"

Molly shook her head, trying not to laugh. The kid was a menace—an absolutely lovable menace. She held out the photo.

"I'd like you to sketch this for me. The same size and style of these." She gestured to the portraits hanging in the stairwell.

Eddie accepted the photo, all teasing and teenage bravado gone. "Who's the dude?"

Frank leaned over Eddie's shoulder, then glanced at Molly. His Adam's apple worked on a slow swallow, his gray eyes soft with emotion and approval.

"His name was Jason North," Molly said softly.

"North?" Lamar asked. "Does he have something to do with North Haven?"

"Yes. Everything, in fact. If it wasn't for him, none of this would be possible."

"Who was he?" Lizzy asked.

"A very special man. You could say he was responsible for bringing Adam and me together."

"When will Adam be back?" Lizzy whispered. "I miss him."

"So do I, honey." They'd agreed to tell the kids that Adam had gone out of town on a family emergency. Actually it *was* a family emergency, because the results of Malcolm Kitoczynski's test would determine whether they *could* be a family.

She refused to consider the downside of the equation.

"What happened to this guy?" Eddie asked, still staring at the photo, his artistic brain formulating just how he'd sketch the likeness.

"He died working for the United States government," Molly said. "He was a man who survived the foster-care system, who made some good choices." She looked at Frank, noticed how he'd slipped his arm around Elena, how he still stared at the picture Eddie held so reverently in his hands.

"With the help of a caring police officer, Jason North turned an underprivileged life-style into something good and respectable and prosperous. Prosperous enough to buy this huge house."

"Did he have to fight on the streets?" Lizzy asked.

"He might have. He grew up in neighborhoods very similar to the ones you kids have."

"Wow."

"Yes," Molly said softly, "wow. And I think his picture belongs right here beside the other ancestors of this house so that we won't ever forget him."

Eddie mounted the stairs and took a closer look at the portraits. Then he turned, placing his hand on Molly's shoulder, his young features taking on a maturity that brought a lump to her throat.

"I'll do him proud, Miss Kincade."

"I know you will, Eddie."

ADAM WENT DIRECTLY to the mansion from the hospital. He overpaid the taxi driver and nearly forgot his duffel bag in his haste to see Molly.

There were changes, even in the three weeks he'd been gone. The house had a lived-in feel to it, a warmth that reached out and engulfed, even though there were no sounds of activity coming from any of the rooms.

With the duffel bag clutched in his hand, he headed up the stairs. He started to call out to Molly, but changed his mind, decided on surprise.

His steps slowed when the portrait caught his eye. Before there had been only five. Now there were six.

He stared at the face, a familiar face from the past, then looked at the brass plate beneath it. Jason North. Founder Of North Haven. 1961–1995.

He remembered when he'd first bought the house, how he'd looked at these pictures on the wall, wondered if anyone would care enough to put *his* up after he was gone.

Molly had cared.

She'd kept him alive with her love, given him a future.

Something inside him gave way, filling him with a peace that banished the last of his loneliness.

"Mr. Walsh?"

He turned at Elena's astonished voice, felt himself smiling like a fool, felt like swooping her in his arms and laughing until the halls rang with his happiness. Elena Martinez had put on some weight in the past three weeks. It looked good on her. She wore an apron over a pretty green dress and had flour on her hands.

Adam realized that the smell wafting from the kitchen was homemade cookies. Ah, what a homecoming. Now all he needed was Molly.

"Hi, Elena. It's good to see you."

"And you, too. Our Molly will be thrilled."

"Is she upstairs?"

Elena shook her head. Just then, Frank came into the room. "Elena, sweetheart, I'm afraid you'll need to whip up another batch of those—" Frank's words ended abruptly. "Adam?" His tanned face split into a wide grin.

"In the flesh."

"Strong as an ox, are you?"

"Not quite. Getting weaker by the minute looking at your mug."

"I take it the emergency's passed? Everyone well and happy and promised a disgustingly long life?"

"Doctors have given the A-OK." Adam met Frank halfway, held out his hand. "Ah, to hell with it." Instead of a handshake, the two men embraced.

"Did I hear you say 'sweetheart'?" Adam questioned dryly, taking care that Elena didn't overhear.

Frank shrugged and gave a wink. "She's a damned good woman. Definitely sweet."

"Is there love on the horizon?"

"Never know. Thought I'd stick around for a while longer, see what develops."

Adam nodded. "I'd like that. I suspect Elena wouldn't object, either." He stepped back. "As much as this turn of events thrills me, I'm a little anxious to take care of my own love life."

Adam glanced at Elena. "Where's Molly?"

"Oh, I believe she's over in the old neighborhood."

Adam's gaze whipped to Frank. "What the hell's she doing there? And why are you *here?*"

Frank shrugged. "She said she didn't need me."

"She *always* says stuff like that. Damn it, Frank, I left you in charge. You were supposed to watch over her!"

Frank just grinned, unperturbed by Adam's hostility. "Since I'm doing such a poor job of it, it's lucky you're home now, isn't it?"

Adam blew out a frustrated breath. "Are the keys to the Porsche in the kitchen?"

"I doubt it." Frank looked at Elena, sharing a grin with her. "Didn't Molly take the Porsche?"

"Yes, I believe she did. She does like to take the T-top section off of it."

Adam wondered if they had all lost their sense while he was gone. "She took my Porsche into the old neighborhood?"

"It's only a car, Adam."

"A hell of an expensive car!" With the sound of Frank's laughter ringing in his ears, Adam headed for the garage, snagging the keys to Molly's Honda on the way.

AT LEAST THERE WAS still daylight left, Adam thought grudgingly, searching for an open parking spot. On a Saturday, though, kids were out of school, probably looking for trouble.

What could she have been thinking?

He wedged the Honda in behind his Porsche, nearly tapping the bumper. Pocketing the keys, he got out and glared at the teenager leaning against the shiny black paint job.

"Touch those tires and you're dead meat," he warned.

The lanky kid with a bandanna tied around his forehead glared right back at Adam. "Ain't nobody touching the tires on this car! Belongs to Miss Kincade. And I'm watchin' it for her."

Great. Hire a gang member to baby-sit his car. "Where is the little spitfire, anyway?"

The kid grinned. "That'd be Miss Kincade you're talkin' 'bout." He gave a toss of his head. "Right across the street, man. Check it out."

And Adam did check it out, his gut doing a series of somersaults when he spotted her.

She was smack in the middle of the baddest, meanest-looking kids Adam had seen in a long time. A five-foot-two dynamo bossing them around as if they were innocent kindergarteners on a field trip. Kids who wore gang colors and towered over her, who could probably snap her like a toothpick.

He decided right then and there that this woman needed a keeper.

When his haze of panic cleared, he noticed that most of the misfit teens were falling all over themselves to do her bidding—which appeared to be cleaning up the neighborhood and ridding it of graffiti, he realized.

Man alive, this woman was something.

His ground-eating strides slowed. There were sketches lying around and buckets of paint—not a spray can in sight. With Molly spearheading the effort, the group was turning rival scrawlings into a mural.

"If you want to express yourselves," he heard Molly say, "use your artistic talents to paint something of beauty, something with meaning, something that makes you proud . . . something you love." Her words lost their commanding tone, taking on an aching softness that got the attention of every young person standing around her.

Including Adam.

"What do *you* love, Miss Kincade?" One of the teenage girls asked.

Adam felt her sadness hit him in strong waves, felt her battle it back—Malcolm had said he'd probably always have a sensitivity to thoughts and emotions. Adam could live with that. As long as it meant he could *live*.

With Molly.

He also felt her eternal hope, one of the very things he admired and loved about her. She never gave up, never backed down or shied away from toughness.

"I love a very special man," Molly said quietly, making Adam's heart soften and swell. "He's a man who's strong and good and noble. A man who brings out the best parts of me. A man who's my strongest weakness."

"Hey, that's an oxymoron."

Molly smiled. "I'm glad to see you're finally paying attention in class, Maria. And that's exactly what he is to me. He simply makes my world stand still. I just wish he'd agree to stand still *with* me in that world."

Aw, hell. How had he gotten so lucky?

"He agrees," Adam said, moving out of the shadows. "And he loves you, too. More than life."

Molly froze, her heart and stomach changing places in a way that robbed her of speech. Slowly, her pulse hammering like the rapid fire of an Uzi, she turned, her heart soaring. Tears welled in her eyes, swift and stinging.

"Adam?"

"I have it on the authority of our nation's top scientists that I can give you babies and forever, Molly Kincade. Or at least forever as far as growing old together entails. Will you marry me? Have my babies? Let me stand still with you in your world?"

Advice buzzed among the teenagers. "Say, yes, Miss Kincade." The shout came from one of the boys.

"Naw, make him wait." A girl spoke this time.

Molly wasn't altogether certain she could pull off a flippant answer. Still, he deserved to sweat for what he'd put her through.

"Well," she hedged, secretly pleased with the way his eyes narrowed—absolutely thrilled that her voice didn't tremble the way her insides did. "A girl can't be too careful these days. Just who is it I'd be growing old with? How do I know it's you?"

His mouth kicked up in a grin that nearly melted Molly right there on the spot. The teenage girls in the group sighed.

He walked toward her slowly, with purpose, the love in his eyes blinding her. Her heart pounded so hard she felt dizzy. She couldn't even meet him halfway. Her legs seemed anchored to the concrete, weighted down with the incredible strength of her emotions. She'd thought she could tease, keep it light. She found that she couldn't.

There was nothing light about her feelings for Adam Walsh.

Kids parted, offered encouragement, then fell silent at the emotion that zinged between the two adults. Adam stopped, reaching out to lightly touch her hair, her temple, the tear that slipped down her cheek.

"I tell a woman I love her, and she asks who I am." He shook his head in mock disappointment.

"Maybe I need to hear it again."

"I love you, Molly Kincade." So softly. "I always have." A whisper now. His thumb swept gently across her lower lip. "Convinced yet?"

Her fingers clutched at the front of his shirt. "It's starting to come back to me," she allowed. "I might warn you, though, the man I intend to grow old with would have to promise never to disappear again...you know, in sickness and in health and all that?"

"I'm sorry, half pint. I was wrong. I wasted a lot of time with self-pity. I should have trusted that you'd be my strength if I ever became weak. You've given me faith because you believed in me. I won't make the mistake of underestimating you again."

She stared at him for several heartbeats, his perfectly sculpted face the most welcome sight she could ever wish for. "And you're positive you're not dying?"

"Yes. At least not from any superhuman stuff."

She nodded, reared back and socked him, eliciting oohs and a "go, girl" from the crowd of teens still watching with avid interest.

"Hey," Adam complained, rubbing his shoulder. "What was that for?"

"I wouldn't dream of hitting a dying man. A healthy one is another matter. How dare you put me through a year of pure hell thinking you were dead!"

He seriously took his newfound life in his hands when he grinned. "Ah, there's the spitfire I know and love. Marry me?"

"I haven't decided if it's really you or not."

"I know a surefire way to prove my identity, half pint."

Oh, yes. Absolutely. "How's that?"

"Kiss me and find out."

And Molly laughed, threw her arms around his neck and held on. Her heart had always known his. Blind or in the deepest darkness of night, she would forever recognize this beautiful, wonderful man by his kiss.

INSTANT WIN 4229 SWEEPSTAKES
OFFICIAL RULES

1. NO PURCHASE NECESSARY. YOU ARE DEFINITELY A WINNER. For eligibility, play your instant win ticket and claim your prize as per instructions contained thereon. If your "Instant Win" ticket is missing or you wish another, send a self-addressed, stamped envelope (WA residents need not affix return postage) to: Instant Win 4229 Ticket, P.O. Box 9045, Buffalo, NY 14269-9045 in the U.S., and in Canada, P.O. Box 609, Fort Erie, Ontario, L2A 5X3. Only one (1) "Instant Win" ticket will be sent per outer mailing envelope. Requests received after 12/30/96 will not be honored.

2. Prize claims received after 1/15/97 will be deemed ineligible and will not be fulfilled. The exact prize value of each Instant Win ticket will be determined by comparing returned tickets with a prize value distribution list that has been preselected at random by computer. Prizes are valued in U.S. currency. For each one million, or part thereof, tickets distributed, the following prizes will be made available: 1 at $2,500 cash; 1 at $1,000 cash; 3 at $250 cash each; 5 at $50 cash each; 10 at $25 cash each; 1,000 at $1 cash each; and the balance at 50¢ cash each. Unclaimed prizes will not be awarded.

3. Winner claims are subject to verification by D. L. Blair, Inc., an independent judging organization whose decisions on all matters relating to this sweepstakes are final. Any returned tickets that are mutilated, tampered with, illegible or contain printing or other errors will be deemed automatically void. No responsibility is assumed for lost, late, nondelivered or misdirected mail. Taxes are the sole responsibility of winners. Limit: One (1) prize to a family, household or organization.

4. Offer open only to residents of the U.S. and Canada, 18 years of age or older, except employees of Harlequin Enterprises Limited, D. L. Blair, Inc., their agents and members of their immediate families. All federal, state, provincial, municipal and local laws apply. Offer void in Puerto Rico, the province of Quebec and wherever prohibited by law. All winners will receive their prize by mail. Taxes and/or duties are the sole responsibility of the winners. No substitution for prizes permitted. Major prize winners may be asked to sign and return an Affidavit of Eligibility within 30 days of notification. Noncompliance within this time or return of affidavit as undeliverable may result in disqualification, and prize may never be awarded. By acceptance of a prize, winners consent to the use of their names, photographs or other likeness for purposes of advertising, trade and promotion on behalf of Harlequin Enterprises Limited, without further compensation, unless prohibited by law. In order to win a prize, residents of Canada will be required to correctly answer a time-limited arithmetical skill-testing question to be administered by mail.

5. For a list of major prize winners (available after 2/14/97), send a self-addressed, stamped envelope to: "Instant Win 4229 Sweepstakes" Major Prize Winners, P.O. Box 4200, Blair, NE 68009-4200, U.S.A.

MILLION DOLLAR SWEEPSTAKES
OFFICIAL RULES
NO PURCHASE NECESSARY TO ENTER

1. To enter, follow the directions published. Method of entry may vary. For eligibility, entries must be received no later than March 31, 1998. No liability is assumed for printing errors, lost, late, non-delivered or misdirected entries.

   To determine winners, the sweepstakes numbers assigned to submitted entries will be compared against a list of randomly, preselected prize winning numbers. In the event all prizes are not claimed via the return of prize winning numbers, random drawings will be held from among all other entries received to award unclaimed prizes.

2. Prize winners will be determined no later than June 30, 1998. Selection of winning numbers and random drawings are under the supervision of D. L. Blair, Inc., an independent judging organization whose decisions are final. Limit: one prize to a family or organization. No substitution will be made for any prize, except as offered. Taxes and duties on all prizes are the sole responsibility of winners. Winners will be notified by mail. Odds of winning are determined by the number of eligible entries distributed and received.

3. Sweepstakes open to residents of the U.S. (except Puerto Rico), Canada and Europe who are 18 years of age or older, except employees and immediate family members of Torstar Corp., D. L. Blair, Inc., their affiliates, subsidiaries, and all other agencies, entities, and persons connected with the use, marketing or conduct of this sweepstakes. All applicable laws and regulations apply. Sweepstakes offer void wherever prohibited by law. Any litigation within the province of Quebec respecting the conduct and awarding of a prize in this sweepstakes must be submitted to the Régie des alcools, des courses et des jeux. In order to win a prize, residents of Canada will be required to correctly answer a time-limited arithmetical skill-testing question to be administered by mail.

4. Winners of major prizes (Grand through Fourth) will be obligated to sign and return an Affidavit of Eligibility and Release of Liability within 30 days of notification. In the event of non-compliance within this time period or if a prize is returned as undeliverable, D. L. Blair, Inc. may at its sole discretion, award that prize to an alternate winner. By acceptance of their prize, winners consent to use of their names, photographs or other likeness for purposes of advertising, trade and promotion on behalf of Torstar Corp., its affiliates and subsidiaries, without further compensation unless prohibited by law. Torstar Corp. and D. L. Blair, Inc., their affiliates and subsidiaries are not responsible for errors in printing of sweepstakes and prize winning numbers. In the event a duplication of a prize winning number occurs, a random drawing will be held from among all entries received with that prize winning number to award that prize.

5. This sweepstakes is presented by Torstar Corp., its subsidiaries and affiliates in conjunction with book, merchandise and/or product offerings. The number of prizes to be awarded and their value are as follows: Grand Prize — $1,000,000 (payable at $33,333.33 a year for 30 years); First Prize — $50,000; Second Prize — $10,000; Third Prize — $5,000; 3 Fourth Prizes — $1,000 each; 10 Fifth Prizes — $250 each; 1,000 Sixth Prizes — $10 each. Values of all prizes are in U.S. currency. Prizes in each level will be presented in different creative executions, including various currencies, vehicles, merchandise and travel. Any presentation of a prize level in a currency other than U.S. currency represents an approximate equivalent to the U.S. currency prize for that level, at that time. Prize winners will have the opportunity of selecting any prize offered for that level; however, the actual non U.S. currency equivalent prize if offered and selected, shall be awarded at the exchange rate existing at 3:00 P.M. New York time on March 31, 1998. A travel prize option, if offered and selected by winner, must be completed within 12 months of selection and is subject to: traveling companion(s) completing and returning of a Release of Liability prior to travel; and hotel and flight accommodations availability. For a current list of all prize options offered within prize levels, send a self-addressed, stamped envelope (WA residents need not affix postage) to: MILLION DOLLAR SWEEPSTAKES Prize Options, P.O. Box 4456, Blair, NE 68009-4456, USA.

6. For a list of prize winners (available after July 31, 1998) send a separate, stamped, self-addressed envelope to: MILLION DOLLAR SWEEPSTAKES Winners, P.O. Box 4459, Blair, NE 68009-4459, USA.

EXTRA BONUS PRIZE DRAWING
NO PURCHASE OR OBLIGATION NECESSARY TO ENTER

7. The Extra Bonus Prize will be awarded in a random drawing to be conducted no later than 5/30/98 from among all entries received. To qualify, entries must be received by 3/31/98 and comply with published directions. Prize ($50,000) is valued in U.S. currency. Prize will be presented in different creative expressions, including various currencies, vehicles, merchandise and travel. Any presentation in a currency other than U.S. currency represents an approximate equivalent to the U.S. currency value at that time. Prize winner will have the opportunity of selecting any prize offered in any presentation of the Extra Bonus Prize Drawing; however, the actual non U.S. currency equivalent prize, if offered and selected by winner, shall be awarded at the exchange rate existing at 3:00 P.M. New York time on March 31, 1998. For a current list of prize options offered, send a self-addressed, stamped envelope (WA residents need not affix postage) to: Extra Bonus Prize Options, P.O. Box 4462, Blair, NE 68009-4462, USA. All eligibility requirements and restrictions of the MILLION DOLLAR SWEEPSTAKES apply. Odds of winning are dependent upon number of eligible entries received. No substitution for prize except as offered. For the name of winner (available after 7/31/98), send a self-addressed, stamped envelope to: Extra Bonus Prize Winner, P.O. Box 4463, Blair, NE 68009-4463, USA.

SWP-H12CF1

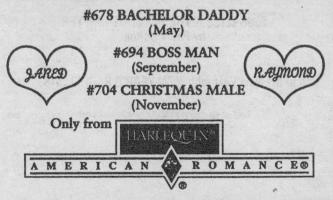

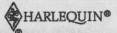

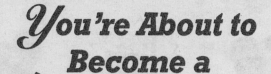

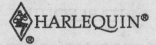